Cornbread and Coffins:
Alphabet Soup Mysteries

Book 3

Erica J Whelton

Publisher: Sunseri Design Publishing
Cover Designer: Mariah Sinclair Book Cover Design
ISBN: 978-1-956069-29-7

Printed in the United States of America

To my grandsons who cheer for me each
time I finish a book.
Thanks for the support boys. Gigi loves you!!

Books in this series:

Appetizers and Alibis (Book 1)
Biscuits and Bodies (Book 2)
Cornbread and Coffins (Book 3)
Dumplings and Disaster (Book 4)
Eclairs and Executions (Book 5)

Other books by this author:

<u>Paranormal Cozy Mystery</u>
Premedicated Murder: Medium with a Heart (book 1)
Replicated Murder: Medium with a Heart (book 2)
Organized Murder: Medium with a Heart (book 3)
Inherited Murder: Medium with a Heart (book 4)
Crafted Murder: Medium with a Heart (book 5)
Destined Murder: Medium with a Heart (book 6)

<u>Small-town Women's Fiction</u>
Mandy's Story: Courage – Finding Herself Series (book 1)
Becca's Story: Purpose – Finding Herself Series (book 2)
Caroline's Story: Serenity – Finding Herself Series (book 3)

The Haunting of Anna-Rose (Paranormal Suspense)
Decoding Us (Women's Fiction/Friendship)

Chapter One

I stood back, watching the mourners fill their plates, chatting solemnly to each other, and nibbling at their food. Granny caught my eye and smiled through a few tears.

Today, I was catering my first and only funeral service. It wasn't what I would have typically thought of or wanted to do. It wasn't part of my business plan, but when your grandmother asks you to do it, you can't say no. So here I am smiling and pointing to the napkins.

My grandmother was a saint. She volunteered as a hospice visitor to those that were alone or had very little family.

This was the service for Lois Dandy, a lady my granny knew from her volunteering work. Lois and Granny had visited, played cards, and watched television together almost daily. They had gotten close the last two months together.

Lois had recently had her hundredth birthday, and had, of course, outlived both her parents, her siblings, two husbands, and both of her daughters. She left behind a son, three grandchildren, five great-grandchildren, and one great-great-grandchild.

Her son, Kyle, was local, but none of the rest of the family lived close. Granny sat with Lois when Kyle was at work, went home to shower, or needed a break.

She passed peacefully about two weeks ago. Granny immediately called me to ask if I would do the catering.

"The funeral home will coordinate and include it as part of the package, if you agree."

"What does that mean, exactly?"

"You would work with and invoice the home, rather than the client. Kyle, Lois's son, has enough to worry about without thinking about one more bill."

I marinated on the thought for all of half a second. Dealing with all the arrangements, her estate, and grieving would be overwhelming and having one less thing to do would be a good thing. Even if my instinct was to say no, I knew that empathy would win out along with Granny's nagging.

"Fine. I'll do it, but this is a one-time thing," I said.

"Sure, Mija, sure."

I knew Granny would wrangle me into it again if this went well, heck even if it didn't, but by the looks of things, it was going well. Everyone was eating, getting seconds, and commenting to each other about how good the food tasted. It made me proud.

I had brought my employees, Shayla and Jordan, to assist me with setting up and serving. Shayla was an apprentice who came to me from the culinary arts high school. I had created a partnership with my old teacher, Mr. Duncan Jones. I had two others from the school who worked for me. Jacoby and Brooklynne had two more years of schooling left, while Shayla had only one.

Shayla was a whiz pastry chef, and I could see a real future for her in this business, even if one day she left me. I plan to offer her a full-time job as soon as she graduates.

There was quite a crowd here for Lois's service, though. When they placed the order, it was for ninety people. Knowing that food can go fast, and people show up who you aren't expecting, I made enough for a hundred people.

Thankfully, I did. As I looked around, this place was standing room only with all seats filled. The funeral home had to bring in a few more, but there were still people without seats.

I hadn't been to many funerals, but I could only hope everyone had such an unexpectedly good turnout.

"Chef, this is a great spread," a lady said.

"Thank you."

"I'd love to book you for an event. Do you have a card?" she asked.

"Oh, I don't really do catering," I smiled.

"Really? What a waste." She tsk-tsked me as she walked away.

Well, that hadn't gone well.

After a few minutes, I was approached by another person asking for catering and then another. I gave the same answer.

"Are you sure?"

"Yes, I am focused on the restaurant."

"That's a shame. You could do so well at this."

I wanted to argue that I was already doing well, but it wasn't worth it. Maybe I should consider catering. It was something to at least think about it.

"Everyone keeps asking about catering," Jordan said, coming up to me.

"I know."

"Are you thinking about it?"

"The restaurant is still new-ish, so I want to keep focused on it."

"Makes sense, but I'd be willing to help if you decide to do it." She grinned and walked off to check the food levels.

I had considered doing a food truck or a booth at the art festivals, but I had never wanted to do catering. This might change my mind, especially if people like Jordan were willing to work for me and support me.

It would just take planning and organization. I'd have to continue to work out the details of it.

Lost in my thoughts, I didn't notice Granny Ines come to stand next to me. She had a plate piled high with my baked ziti, pasta salad, and a cucumber sandwich. That was just a small selection of what we'd brought.

"You look lost in thought." She chuckled. "Everything okay?"

"Oh, yes, just thinking."

"Everyone loves your food. I'm so proud of you."

"Thanks. I'm glad I did it."

"See, Granny might know a thing or two about business."

"Well, I learned from the best."

My Papa Vincent had run his own furniture business. He'd passed away when I was still a baby, so I don't remember him. After he passed, Granny and Uncle Sully kept it going. Apparently, she'd been a shrewd businesswoman.

Then when my dad went to prison, she sold her shares of the business to Uncle Sully. Between what she and Papa Vincent had saved and the sale, she'd had enough money to live out her life and care for me.

Growing up, she taught me how to stretch a dollar, how to keep a house, and how to cook. The things I wish I'd learned better were courage and confidence. She was one of the strongest women I knew and had both in abundance.

Granny walked away to speak to someone else. I started walking around, collecting trash, checking with my employees, and double-checking food.

Gio Caruso, the owner of the funeral home, came over to greet us.

"Chef, how's it going?"

"Good, I think."

"Well, I have heard good things."

"Ah, well, thank you." I smiled. "I was told to bring our invoice with me. Do I give that to you?"

"Oh, no, no. I'm heading to our other facility now. Give it to Donna in the office."

"Okay, thanks."

He walked away, waving as he went out the front door. After that, we waited for things to wind down.

"Jessie? Little Jessie Vasquez, is that you?" a tiny woman said. Her white hair was cut in a pixie style. She had dark pink blush on her cheeks, bright blue eyeshadow, and cherry red lipstick. The haircut and thick makeup made her look like an old fairy.

"Oh, hi, Ms. Lolly."

"You remember me?"

"Of course. I saw you a few years ago at Granny's birthday party."

She had been a long-time friend of the family, and once upon a time, my babysitter. I had always thought she had fairy-like features, but as she'd aged, it was more noticeable.

She was also part of my grandmother's Bible study group, though I rarely saw them these days. I would run into this one or that at the grocery store or around town, but it had been some time since I had seen Ms. Lolly.

"Oh, good, you do remember me! How are you, dear?"

"I'm good. How are you?"

"I'm doing okay. You know I lost my sweet Ray last year."

"Yes, I am so sorry. He was a good man."

"He thought the world of you. We would cheer and pray for you when you'd compete. He would clip the news articles and stick them on our fridge."

"That's so sweet. Thank you."

"I heard you catered the funeral. The food was lovely. I haven't gotten to make it out to your restaurant yet, but I would like to."

"I'd love to have you come see us. Let me know if you are there. I work mostly the lunch shift."

"I will come by soon." She leaned up to hug me.

Hugging her, she felt so frail compared to the last time I saw her, which was six years ago for Granny Ines's sixty-fifth birthday party. She had always been a small woman, but she used to feel so solid. One of those mighty but strong types. I kept that observation to myself.

"It was good to see you, Miss Lolly."

"Good to see you too, dear." She made her way around the room, greeting others.

I hadn't realized that she knew Lois, but it's possible that she had met her through Granny. They had remained good friends since they were schoolgirls, both marrying their high school sweethearts and attending the same church. I heard they used to vacation together before my papa got sick.

I first met them at Sunday dinners at Granny's house. Then they would babysit me. They loved children and would babysit many of their friends' children. I loved going to their house because I got to play with the other kids.

The funeral guests started to leave, thanking us on their way out. A few grabbed items to-go. If I had thought about it, I would have brought containers for that.

Once most had left, my team and I started cleaning up. About halfway through, I decided it was time to go drop the invoice with Donna Overton.

"Okay, y'all have the rest?" I asked them.

"Yes, Chef," Jordan said.

Shayla simply nodded. I'd found she was a girl of few words.

"Alrighty, then I'm going to see if I can find the assistant to leave the invoice with. Back in a minute."

Gio had said in the office, but I really hoped I could find her without having to go down the creepy hallway.

I was ready to be out of here. It was an eerie place with old, dated wallpaper that felt like it came out of a horror movie. There were statues and portraits on the wall with eyes that appeared to follow your every move. The marble floors seemed to echo my steps against the empty hall.

I stuck my head in the first room. The door was open, so I thought I'd take a chance that Donna would be in here.

It looked like a showroom, with caskets displayed around the room with the prices and features listed on each. There was another wall with a glass case that housed urns. A shiver ran down my back.

I continued to the next room. It said office, but the door was shut. I knocked.

No answer.

I walked down to the end of the hallway, but the only door down here said morgue. No way was I going in there. I went back to the office door and knocked again.

When again there was no answer, I decided to try the door. It wasn't locked, so I pushed the door open.

"Hello? Donna?"

That's when I saw her. Donna Overton lying on the floor. I knew without going to her what I would find.

She was dead.

"Not again," I muttered.

Chapter Two

The police arrived, including Officer Kyle Rafferty and Officer Tommy Roberts. They were the ones that usually arrived first. Detective Upton would likely be close behind.

"Well, Jess, what has happened here?" Raff asked with a chuckle.

"So unprofessional, Raff." I said. "A lady died."

"I know, but why do we keep running into you at these calls?"

"Bad luck?"

"And now you know why I laughed."

"Anyway, to answer your question, I was looking for Donna, so I could leave the invoice for the catering. When I got to the office, she was on the floor."

"Um, okay. Stay close. We're going to start interviews and investigating."

I plopped into one of the chairs and looked over at Jordan and Shayla. I felt so bad that they were now stuck while we waited for the police to release us. In my experience, this could be hours.

Granny Ines came over, taking a seat next to me, patting my leg.

"What did they say?"

"We have to wait until they question most everyone. Since I found her, I assume that is why they want me here." I honestly didn't know. "Did they talk to you yet?"

"Yeah, just a moment ago. Said I could go. I'm just waiting for Margarita to get here." She had always called Aunt Rita by her full name, while everyone else called her by her nickname. "Do you need anything, Mija?"

I wanted to say I needed to stop being involved with dead people, but it seemed an almost selfish thought. I just said nothing. She kissed my cheek, then went to wait for Rita outside.

Gio came bursting in. He ran through the hallway to the office. The officers kept him in the hallway, so I was able to hear him. His booming voice demanded answers.

"I need to know what happened!"

"We don't know yet, but we are trying to figure that out."

"Can I see her at least?" His normally booming voice cracked.

"Okay," Rafferty said, stepping to the side.

A choking sob traveled down the hallway. My heart broke for him. I know what it felt like to lose my own employee. I felt responsible for him and all my employees.

He came out, head in his hand. He looked my way, giving a weak smile and then turning towards the morgue. I assumed he was going to wait there.

Hours passed. I watched as they released person after person, including my staff, while asking me to remain behind.

"We'll get everything back to the restaurant and clean up, don't worry, Chef." Jordan had assured me before they left.

I couldn't help but worry about why I was asked to wait here. It wasn't like I saw anything or knew anything. While I waited, I heard Roberts tell Raff that the coroner's office was on their way. I hadn't been on a scene like this before when they came for the body. With Earl, they'd loaded me into a patrol car and taken me to the station. Then with Colt, I'd come to the scene later but was not involved.

"Jess, hey," someone said.

I looked up to see a face I hadn't seen in years. It was like the day of reunions, but I guess since I wasn't traveling as much and was getting out of the restaurant more, it was bound to happen.

"Wow, hi, Max. It's been a while."

We had gone to school together from preschool until tenth grade when I moved over to the Culinary Arts school where I graduated. I'd only kept in touch with Sawyer and Vee from school days.

I occasionally ran into him, like many of my classmates, but our conversations were aways brief. Just a hello and how are you, then bye.

"It has. You look great."

"So do you."

"Are you involved in this thing?" He thumbed behind him.

"Um, I was catering a service and found her body." I winced at the words.

"Oh, dang." He looked over his shoulder. Lowering his voice, he continued. "Well, let me see if I can figure out what the cause is. We might not know immediately."

He waved as he made his way down the hallway to the office.

I watched him as he ducked into the room. Voices drifted down the hall, but by the time they reached me, I couldn't make out any words.

Honestly, I didn't care what they had to say, I just wanted to go home.

It was another hour before Rafferty came over to me.

"Initial cause of death. Poisoning."

From crime shows, I knew that there were sometimes signs on the body, like foaming at the mouth or blue lips and skin. It would depend on the type of poison what her symptoms would present.

"Poisoning?" I choked out the word.

"Yeah, so we need to look at the food you had. Where is it?"

"Jordan and Shayla took it back to the restaurant."

"Why did they leave?"

"Y'all said they could."

"Crap, that was before—" He looked around.

"Let me call them to see if they can bring it all back up here."

Though I imagine they had it all cleaned up by now.

"Actually, no, let's all go over. We'll need to gather evidence and take pictures. All of that."

"Do you want me to call to make sure they don't throw anything out yet?"

"Yes, but don't tell them why."

I hit the button for Jordan.

"Hey, Chef, what's up?"

"Do y'all still have the food from today?"

"Um, most of it, but not all."

"Okay, I'm coming over there now. Please save the rest and don't do anything until I get there."

"Um, okay, I assume this has to do with the dead lady?"

"Yeah, something like that." I was careful to keep my voice neutral. Rafferty didn't want them to know the reason, and I'm sure that was so that they didn't tamper with anything. Though I knew the food was fine.

"Okay, see you soon."

I hung up and looked at Raff. "They still have the food. We can head over when you're ready."

"She knows why we want it, huh?"

I thought about lying to him, but there really was no point. He knew that she knew.

"Yeah."

"Then we need to go."

"Do you mind if I ride with you? They were my ride."

"Yeah, Chief wants me to keep an eye on you, anyway."

"On me, why?"

"You know why."

"I don't, actually." Crossing my arms hard over my chest.

"Don't make me say it, please. You know I cheer for you, but she was poisoned. It had to be in her food."

"I never saw her out here eating the food. She had been working the entire time. Gio did eat some food before he left, but not her."

"Well, nonetheless, we need to check the food. We have already gathered everything in the office, so your food is next."

"Alrighty."

We waited for Roberts to join us, then they had me sit in the backseat. I felt humiliated sitting there as if I was under arrest, even though I knew I wasn't. Anyone who saw me in the car wouldn't know though, so I tried to keep my head down.

They tried to make small talk with me on the way over, but my mind wasn't into it. All I could think about was another murder. Another murder.

Bleep!

How could they suspect me in this? I barely knew Donna and had nothing against her. We had worked together the past week to get the menu set for this service, but that was the limit of my interaction with her.

Without knowing anything about her, I couldn't even speculate who could have done it. Was it Gio? Even though he had seemed upset over her death, had they fought over ... well, I don't know, something funeral home business? Could it be an ex-boyfriend or ex-girlfriend? An old friend? A rival? I had no idea and no way to know at this point.

The only thing I did know for sure is that I didn't do it.

As we neared my restaurant, my stomach fluttered. This felt so unreal.

"You can park in the back," I said.

I didn't want to draw too much attention to myself, even though the parking lot was visible to all of Brush Avenue. Dr. Vega's office had a clear view. He was the optometrist across the road from us.

He probably thought of us as his crazy neighbors since we have had to get security footage from them a few times. I had started to send them free lunch once a week as a thank you. It was a small price to pay to keep our neighbors happy.

We headed into the restaurant via the back door.

Things were hopping inside, but I saw that Shayla and Jordan had everything still on carts by the back door. Jordan came over, nodding to the two carts loaded with leftover food and all the containers we had transported it in.

Raff and Roberts put on gloves and evidence bags, then got to work.

I stood back, arms crossed, watching them work. They worked with only a few words spoken, only what was necessary to make notes and label the evidence.

Next, Roberts took out his phone and began taking pictures of the food. Not sure what he hoped to determine from that, but whatever they needed, if it proved my staff and I were innocent.

"Alrighty, Jess, I think that's all we need," Raff said, giving me a salute. "We'll be in touch if we need anything else."

"Thanks." I held the door open, watching them walk out to their car, then I stood there watching them drive away.

It was only then that I exhaled. At least I wasn't arrested or even taken into the station. I turned towards my staff. "Well, this sucks."

Chapter Three

I woke up after a sleepless night. Laying there, I just stared at the ceiling for a few moments, then rolled to my side to stare at my favorite two pieces of art. One was bought from a local artist who turned out to be working with others to sabotage my business. Despite the artist, I loved the little elfin boy that I'd nicknamed Luca.

Next to Luca was a dragon which I'd gotten from April Evans. Her brother Colt had been killed on his way to meet me for a blind date. Colt and I never got to meet, but April thought Colt would want me to have this dragon and some of his t-shirts.

They were actually Neal Barney shirts. He was a local artist who did folklore art and put it on shirts, purses, and canvas. My roommates and I were his biggest fans.

I put the dragon next to Luca. They made me happy, even if there were slightly bad memories attached to them.

Sighing, I pushed myself up. The last two days had been heavy. Why was I involved in another murder investigation? This one pointed to a poisoning and that pointed to my catered food.

I was unable to clear my name until the investigators determined the exact poison she had consumed, then compared it to the food samples they'd gathered.

Well, there were a few things I could do, but Detective Upton had once again warned me to not do any of them. We were standing in the parking lot of my restaurant yesterday after Rafferty and Roberts finished gathering evidence when he issued the warning.

"Look at what happened last time?" He pointed to my new car.

I simply nodded.

It wasn't like I could argue. He was right and didn't need to finish his thought for me to know exactly what he was referring to. Just a few weeks ago, my previous car had been blown up when I was investigating a case of embezzlement. The bad guys didn't want me to keep looking into things. Not sure if they meant to kill me or scare.

Luckily for me, they only succeeded in one of those things.

Though I had a few not-yet-healed burns as a reminder. They were a pale pink now and not the burned flesh of a few weeks ago. They still itched like crazy.

In fact, as I thought about being pulled into a murder again, they began burning. It was like my body wanted to remind me of my past mistakes.

Chief Stone had shown me a lot of appreciation and thanked me for helping them solve the high school's embezzlement scandal recently. But that short-lived appreciation was gone now that I was the prime suspect in this case.

Well, maybe it wasn't just me, but the restaurant's food and my reputation had been called into question. If customers believed that we had something to do with poor Donna's death, it could really hurt my business.

While I lay there pondering my current situation, Lulu jumped up on the bed, climbing onto my chest. She looked down as if she was a queen atop her throne and I was just a peasant. It made me giggle.

"Good morning, Lulu."

She meowed down at me.

"You want food?"

She meowed again, then jumped to the ground, running to her bowl. I followed, dumping a scoop of her dried kibble in the bowl, then ran my hand from head to tail as she dug into her tuna medley.

This is why I loved having a cat. She gave me a reason to get out of bed even on days I was struggling. I smiled down at her as I stepped into the bathroom. I splashed water on my face and then ran a brush through my straight hair.

Simple.

I headed downstairs for some coffee, and perhaps I would make breakfast. Today I was off, Parker was working the day shift and June would be working the evening one.

Having the two extra chefs available to take on the head role had freed me up to have an actual personal life. In fact, I was nearly ready to promote my lead line chef, Hannah, to sous chef as well.

This would give us four people in the top kitchen position and would open a spot for one of the apprentices to take. Shayla would be graduating in December as an early graduate, and with her extensive experience, she was my first choice.

Our other two apprentices, Jacoby and Brooklynne, wouldn't graduate until next year, so by then we might have a position for them.

I took a long sip of coffee as I prepped breakfast. I popped the bacon into the oven. Then, I started grabbing ingredients for pancakes, mixing it into a sweet batter. I let that sit while I got the skillet ready. I had a nice flat one that was perfect for pancakes.

Once the pan was hot, I ladled the batter on and watched it sizzle just slightly. It was magical.

"Perfect."

Flip, flip. Then, once I was satisfied, I took them out. I was about eight pancakes in when Sawyer and Vee made their way downstairs, both dressed for another day at the post office.

"What smells so good?" she asked, before she came fully into the kitchen.

"Pancakes and bacon. Help yourselves." I pointed to the two plates. One piled with perfectly cooked bacon and then the other with a stack of fluffy pancakes. I loved creating beauty with food. "There is more where that came from, too, so eat up."

"Didn't sleep well?" Vee asked, as she got two pancakes.

"You always know," I exhaled, turning to face her. "No, I tossed and turned. This latest murder ... Ugh!"

"Well, obviously the evidence is going to show it wasn't you, so why worry?" She shoveled a large bite of pancake in her mouth.

"I'm with Vee. You're worrying too much when you know you didn't do it."

"Y'all are so right. Why am I so worried?"

Honestly, I was afraid to turn out like my father, which was a silly thought. While I liked to help the underdogs, I wasn't quick to violence like he was.

When I was five years old, he killed a man in front of me. It wasn't until a few months ago that I remembered the reason, but regardless of why, he had a hot temper. It had never been pointed at me or my mother, but he was quick to defend others with violence first, words second.

I loved that he wanted to protect others from bullies, but it got him in trouble so many times in prison. I remember missing visits with him because of fights he'd gotten in, which meant losing his visitation for that month.

In my early teen years, I'd lashed out by sneaking out, egging houses, and other rebellious but mostly harmless teen pranks. Sawyer and Vee were there with me or maybe for me.

Sawyer had an okay home life, but his dad was a long-haul trucker. That just meant he was gone a lot. His mom worked a lot, so Sawyer had a lot of unsupervised time.

Vee had a mostly privileged life, but she wanted so badly to be a rebel and disobey. It usually didn't end up that way. Her parents simply 'talked' to her, and all was forgiven.

I looked at them now. Had they not been my friends, no telling how life would have turned out for me. I had felt so alone most of my growing up years, even with the support of my granny and aunt. They were the ones who raised me.

There were the children at Ms. Lolly's but those kids weren't friends outside of her house. They were just people to play with sometimes and by the time I was a young teenager, I wasn't going there any longer.

"So, what're your plans for the day, Jess?"

"I have to go over to Caruso Funeral Home so I can get paid for the catering job. I wasn't able to leave the invoice last time."

"Why didn't you email them or mail it?"

"They asked for it this way. I have no idea why."

"No paper trail," Sawyer said, taking a bite of bacon.

"What?" Vee and I said in unison.

"Y'all watch the same crime shows I do." he looked at us as if we should know what he meant. When we didn't catch on, he sighed. "Where are they always storing and laundering money?"

Again, we stared at him, unblinking.

He continued. "Places that take in a lot of cash, like strip clubs, laundry mats. But also, funeral homes because even though they don't take a lot of cash, they have enormous expenses, like caskets and things. What better way to explain having large sums of money in the bank?"

"Why does that make perfect sense and yet sound so crazy at the same time?" I said.

"Right?" He chuckled. "If you give them a paper copy, they don't have an electronic copy of the receipt and they can fudge their accounting. Hide things they don't want seen."

"Maybe that's why Donna was killed," Vee blurted.

"Maybe."

That gave me something to think about as I dressed later. Originally, I hadn't even questioned why they wanted me to give them a printed copy and not email it. Now that was all I could think about.

I'd have to ask Noah his thoughts on it later. He had more experience with accounts payable and receivable. I was only managing this since it was a deal coordinated by my granny, not exactly through the restaurant.

I steered my new car across town to the funeral home. I was still getting used to it. It was nice and all, but my other car and I had history. Sure, this one had all the latest features, like an incredible back up camera, moon roof, and heated seats. And sure, it had that amazing new car smell, and nothing was sticky from Vee's ice cream drips or my coffee oopsies.

I looked down at the gorgeous, not yet worn gray seats with the blue stitching that perfectly matched the exterior paint. I ran a hand over the smooth, clean dashboard.

"Who am I kidding? I love this car," I shouted, then laughed at myself.

I turned the radio up loudly and sang along until I steered into the funeral home parking lot. There were about half a dozen cars. I looked at each of them, a habit I was starting to get into. Looking at my surroundings and taking in the little details.

I recognized Gio's car right off. It was a corvette with plates that read CARUSO. I didn't know much about him, other than his family had owned this funeral home for two generations. He was the second Caruso to be in charge.

Rumor was that his son Dimitri did not want to take over. He wanted to be a sculptor. Gio's daughter Talia was married with young children and had expressed openly that she had no desire to take over.

That left all the work to Gio for now, unless one of his children changed their minds, or if Talia's husband took over. But the rumor was Gio didn't want it out of the family control like that. As it was, he had made the poor man sign a prenup to marry Talia.

The door chime announced my arrival as I stepped inside. Right in front of me was the spot that just a few days ago, I sat waiting for the police to tell me my fate. Would they charge me or let me go?

Well, they didn't arrest me, so that was good, but I wasn't off the hook yet.

As I walked down the hallway, the statues and pictures still creeped me out as their eyes followed me. I stopped when Gio came out of the back room.

"Oh, hello, Chef Jessica. Welcome," Gio said, smiling. His booming, friendly voice filled the room and pushed the eerie feeling away. "Are you here with the invoice?"

"Yes, I have it right here."

He stepped forward, taking it from me. I'd met him a few times growing up because I'd gone to school with both his children and they both spent time at Lolly and Ray's, too.

He seemed like a much larger man back then, or maybe it was just because I'd been younger. I stood at six feet tall and now towered over him by about six inches. But despite his shorter stature, he didn't appear like a small man. I'm not sure if it was his weight or his confidence, but he seemed much larger.

"This looks good. Alrighty, follow me. I'll have Regina cut you a check."

"Oh, your wife is working here now?"

"She is. Begrudgingly, but losing Donna really left me in a bind and Dimitri won't get his head out of his … um, behind long enough to help me out here. Wants to be an artist. Can you believe that?"

I wanted to argue and say he was already a great artist, but I knew that wasn't the answer that Gio wanted. I hadn't really seen much of Dimitri's work, except a few pictures online. It wasn't enough to really comment.

Dimitri would likely never be rich or make enough to support himself the way his father had, but if it made him happy, I say go for it.

But to keep the peace, I simply agreed with him..

We stepped into the office where Regina was cursing at the computer.

"This stupid thing froze up on me again," she growled, hitting the side of the outdated monitor. "This piece of ... Oh, hi, Jessica, I didn't see you there."

She stood with a smile. She was close to my height and rumor was she used to be a model before marrying Gio and having two children back-to-back.

Her bouffant hair was colored to a perfect platinum blond. She had an 80s style suit with pleated skirt and shoulder pads in the jacket. She was quite lovely but outdated and out of place in this modern world.

Actually, looking around at the antiquated office with dark wood paneling and heavy wooden furniture, she fit right in.

"Hi, Ms. Regina, how are you?"

"I'm well, dear." She smiled. "How can we help you today?"

"She's brought the invoice for Lois Costello's funeral. The food bill," Gio said, handing over the bill. "You got this?"

"Yeah, I got it, Hun. Thanks!"

"Alrighty, I'm going to go back to prep ... well, for tomorrow's service." With that, he turned and left.

"Great, great. I heard good things about the food, well, except what happened to poor Donna." Regina started typing on the computer, cursing it a few times and then typing again. "I didn't trust that Donna, though. There was something fishy about her and the way she would flirt with my Gio. I had to always come in here and make sure she knew he was mine." She stopped typing as an ancient printer came to life.

It squealed and screeched before spitting out the page.

"Any idea who would want her dead?" If Regina was going to spill everything, I might as well be bold and ask.

"Aren't you inquisitive?" She laughed. It was a trill laugh, like a flock of tiny birds. She wiggled her finger for me to come closer as she lowered her voice. "I hate to speak ill of the dead, but let me just tell you, any man that came in this place, especially if they were married, she would be all over them. Cooing and flirting. Openly flirting with the wife right there if you can believe that."

"Anyone in particular stick out?"

She stood, wobbling on her high heels as she went to the printer, grabbed the check and then brought it back. She signed it quickly, then handed it to me.

"There were a few people. Darcy Whittaker *hated* Donna. They had a huge graveside fight, complete with hair pulling, slapping, and police hauling them both off to the station. It was quite a scene. I was so thankful I was there for it."

"Oh, my." I remember hearing a bit of that through the town gossip channels, namely my Aunt Rita. She was plugged into all the best gossip.

My mom is another good source for gossip, but I wasn't speaking to her at the moment. Not after they went on another family vacation without me. It was like she only remembered she had a daughter when she wanted something from me.

Plus, mom's gossip was almost never true because she would get the facts mixed up.

"Yeah, it was quite the scene. Then, oh, let me think." She leaned forward again. "There was another time with Tilly Franco. They had a shouting match right out in the lobby while we were having a wake for Old Man Marlowe. His widow came running out, all four feet nothing of her, swinging her handbag at them and telling them how disrespectful they were. I can't argue with that. It was disrespectful."

She waved her hands wildly through the entire story. I could barely keep up with her energy, but I tried.

"Marlowe. Lolly Marlowe?"

"Yeah, you know her?"

"She used to babysit me. She and my grandmother are friends."

"Oh yeah, she used to babysit Dimitri and Talia, too."

"Yes, I remembered playing with them." I smiled.

"She could probably tell you all kinds of stories about Donna. You should reach out to her."

"I might just. Well, thanks for this. It was good to see you again."

"Don't be a stranger now. I always thought you and Talia should have stayed friends. I just don't know whatever happened there."

"Oh, you know, people change and grow." The truth was, Talia turned into one of those mean girls. I was her prime target of hate. Her mom didn't need to know that though and it was water under the bridge. We were adults and she was a mom now.

I ran into her a year ago. She was so frazzled by her children, that she barely looked like herself. The dark circles under her eyes, wrinkles in her clothes, and extra weight was not the Talia that I remembered. The Talia I remembered was always put together, like off a magazine cover. She had at least smiled and said it was good to see me.

"Ah, well, take care, dear." She got back to typing on and cursing at the computer.

I thought about what she said about Donna's reputation. Could that be what got her killed? I'd have to ask Aunt Rita and possibly reach out to Ms. Lolly. I didn't know Tilly Franco or Darcy Whittaker well enough to ask them.

They were both in the ible study with Aunt Rita and Granny and I'd only met them a few times. Not close enough to ask such personal questions without a good reason or opportunity.

Tilly ran a boutique jewelry shop. Vee likely knew her. I'd have to ask her. Darcy was the librarian at the elementary school. With no children in school, I had no reason to talk to her. At least there was no reason I could think of now, but I'm sure I would come up with something.

Chapter Four

As I was leaving the Caruso's, I noticed Gio loading a large bag into a dark van. It caught my attention, because of the way he looked around as he did it. Unfortunately for him, he didn't look my way, so he didn't know I noticed.

That was suspicious, right?

However, I didn't know the funeral home business, perhaps that's how he always did stuff. I know I had gotten a lot more paranoid lately, so I looked around more than usual. I tried to take in more details about my surroundings or see if anyone was watching me.

Even though I made a mental note about him, I shrugged off Gio's behavior as I climbed into my car. Checking the time, I had an idea about how to get some more information.

I hit the call button on my car's dashboard.

"Hello, Jessie!" came my Auntie Rita singsong voice through the car speakers.

"Hi, Auntie Rita. Are you busy?"

"No, not at all. I volunteered this morning. Now home doing some chores."

"Want to go to lunch?"

"Oh, yes, I'd love to!"

"Great. I can swing by and pick you up in about twenty minutes."

"I'll be ready!"

We hung up. I smiled. Even if I was using her a little to get some information, I knew this would make her happy. We used to spend a lot more time together, but since I opened the restaurant, I hadn't had as much time. This was going to be a fun lunch and if it helped me solve a murder, that was just gravy.

I drove across town, pulling up at the curb of the familiar craftsman home. Aunt Rita was on the porch in her plaid vintage sundress and tan sandals with wide heels. She was beautiful. I could picture her as a young woman waiting on a date or to go out with friends. It was a shame that she had never married.

Her one that got away was now married in Florida. My one that got away had been murdered two months ago, or at least that's how I now thought of Colt. Having gotten to know him while investigating his murder, we had a lot in common. Who knows what would have happened had he not been murdered?

I sighed and then got out of the car just as my aunt neared it. I opened the door for her, causing her to giggle.

"Oh, Jessie, aren't you a sweetie? But I can still open my own door, I'm not old yet." She winked, then kissed my cheek.

"I know you can, but just being nice." I closed her door, then jogged around to the driver's side. "Any place you would like to go?"

"What about Dashwood Teahouse?"

"How did I know you would say that?" I chuckled as we pulled away from the curb.

"Because you know I love their strawberry spinach salad with grilled chicken."

"They have the best salad dressing," I said.

It was a honey lemon vinaigrette that I had not been able to copy. I just wanted it for my home use, not for the restaurant. Though I'd come close to getting it right, it wasn't Dashwood Teahouse good. Betty, the owner, was very tight-lipped about her recipe. I didn't blame her at all.

"So, why the sudden interest in lunch with your old aunt?"

"I finally had a day off and no murder to investigate."

I didn't mention that's what I was doing. She didn't need to know. I felt a little ping of guilt lying to her, but I also really wanted to spend time with her, and this was the perfect excuse. Two birds, one stone as they say.

I cut my eyes to look at her from the corners, just to see if she bought my little lie. She was smiling brightly and bouncing slightly in her seat. As an ex-dancer, she was always moving to some unheard beat.

"Well, aren't I lucky to get one of your rare days off then?"

We pulled into Dashwood's Teahouse. It was not too far from my restaurant, but I had never felt in competition with her or any of the other restaurants. This was a foodie town, so there was enough business to go around.

Plus, the chefs and owners all supported each other and tried to eat at each other's places. I know I tried to do my part when I was off.

"Jess! Rita! Welcome," Betty said when we stepped inside. "It's so good to see you ladies here today."

"Hi, Betty. It's nice to see you, too," Rita said. I watched as the two ladies did a quick cheek kiss-hug hello.

"Where is Ines today?" Betty asked.

"Oh, she's having lunch over at the senior center with some of our Bible study group."

"That's nice. Table for two, then?"

"Yes, thank you."

We followed her to a two-person bistro style table. It had fresh daisies in a pink pot on the table. We took our seats as she laid pink gingham cloth napkin bundles in front of each of us, then handed us menus.

"Enjoy, ladies." She smiled, walking back to the front door to greet the next guests. As she left, a waitress came over to take our order.

"We actually know what we want, if you're ready?" Aunt Rita told the waitress.

"Oh, perfect." She took out her notepad. "What'll ya have, Hun?"

We both ordered the strawberry spinach salad with grilled chicken.

"Great. I'll bring out your drinks and a basket of cornbread."

We smiled as she walked away.

"That's what you should serve at your place, too. The biscuits are great, but I love a good cornbread muffin."

"I should. Maybe that would be a good project for the students. I could ask them to come up with a recipe and then I'll have the rest of the staff vote on their favorite."

"That's such a good idea! I'm so glad I helped." She ginned.

The waitress returned with our iced teas and a basket of cornbread. They made them in mini muffin pans, which was a wonderful size. They served them with honey butter. I would have to see what the students came up with and then how we would present it. This was going to be a fun project. I couldn't wait to get to work tomorrow to set the wheels in motion.

We each grabbed a muffin and slathered it with the delicious butter. The first bite was so good. A touch sweet and a bit savory.

"This is excellent."

"It is." Auntie Rita smiled. "So, what have you been up to besides working?"

"Not much. This morning, I had to go back over to Caruso's for Lois's funeral."

"Such a shame about Donna, but I'm not surprised. She was always causing trouble, flirting with men, upsetting the wives or girlfriends."

Here we go. She was going to spill it and I wouldn't even have to probe much.

"That's what Ms. Regina said. That's crazy."

"Oh, the stories I could tell, but I won't speak ill of the dead." She took a bite of her muffin.

Bleep! I might have to get her talking after all.

"I understand that, but I know Ms. Regina mentioned a thing with Lolly at Ray's funeral. Were you there?"

She looked around, then made the sign of the cross.

"Yes, I was there. I thought—," She stopped and pointed at me. "*Oh wait*, you were at that one big cooking tournament when Ray passed." She looked around, then giggled slightly. This must be some good gossip. "Anyway, we are there listening to the service. Lolly's daughter, Diane, was speaking and there was all this commotion in the hallway. We tried to ignore it. "

"Diane tried to keep going, but soon it was too much. Lolly stood up and marched right out there. We followed. That's when we saw Tilly Franco and Donna rolling around, and Lolly was yelling and whacking them with her handbag. It was a sight. Alex had to pick up his mom and take her back into the viewing room while the police dealt with Tilly and Donna."

Alex was Lolly and Ray's son. He had been married twice and divorced twice. As far as I knew, he was currently single. He lived in Pinehurst which was a large nearby city.

Many people lived in Dashwood and commuted to the metropolitan area to work. Unless you were in the arts or town government, there was limited work in Dashwood.

"Do you know what Tilly and Donna were fighting about?"

"Tilly was yelling about Donna sleeping with her husband, and Donna was yelling back that she never would."

"Wow, so what happened? Did they ever determine if Donna slept with Tilly's husband?"

"No, he denied it, too, but honestly, nobody believes it. That Donna, may she rest in peace, was always flirting with any man that was near her."

I didn't know how to respond, so I just ate another cornbread muffin.

"Did she tell you about Darcy Whittaker and Donna?" Auntie Rita asked, looking around again to see if anyone was listening. Nobody seemed to be.

"No, what happened?" I whispered.

Ms. Regina had in fact mentioned their fight, but I wanted to hear my aunt's version.

"Again, I hate to speak ill of the dead, *but* we all gathered for Darcy's mother's funeral. Here comes Donna, shaking her moneymaker, prancing back and forth in front of all the men. She said she was just doing her job, but anyone could see she was looking for attention. Darcy was already upset about her mom and when Donna went to say something to her, Darcy just lost it. Now, I didn't hear what started it, but I did see these two sixty-year-old women slapping each other and pulling hair. Donna's dress got ripped and Darcy lost her hairpiece."

Auntie Rita paused when the waitress brought our salads.

"How does everything look?" Our server asked.

"Looks good," I said.

"Great. Do you want more cornbread?" She pointed to the basket.

"Um, no, I think we are good."

She nodded and walked to the next table.

"Okay, where was I?" Aunt Rita continued. "Oh, yes, the police got called and in the process of trying to break them up, the officer was elbowed. Broke his nose. That's when they ended up down at the station. They both had to do six months of community service. They did not like each other at all."

"That's crazy."

"Those are the most memorable and honestly, Darcy, Tilly, and Lolly would be the people who hated Donna the most." She paused, then lowered her voice again. "Oh my gosh, do you think one of them killed Donna?"

"I don't know. Something to think about."

"Maybe you should start using that board that Roy Hart built for y'all."

Roy Hart was Sawyer's father. He had built us a large clue board while I was investigating Colt's death a few months ago. We had used it to put our suspects and clues on. I don't know if it had helped solve his murder, but it had put everything in one place. I think that part was helpful.

"I might do that."

"Just be more careful this time." She patted my hand. "I can help if you want. I am in that circle of ladies. In fact, Tilly and Darcy were in my class back in school. We are also in the same Bible study group. Our next meeting is tomorrow. Then we'll have our larger group later in the week."

"Oh, oh, okay. Let me know if you find anything."

"I will." She giggled. "I can see why you like this. It's exciting."

I wanted to argue that I didn't like it, but if I were honest with myself, there was a little thrill in chasing the clues.

Growing up, I had always enjoyed mystery books. They were still my go-to. I loved true crime shows and any of the police dramas. It was something that I shared with my best friends.

Still, if I never saw another dead body, I'd be happy.

We finished our salads, then each ordered a slice of gingerbread and Earl Grey tea. We got off the topic of fighting, drama, and murder.

She caught me up on family news, especially about my Uncle Sully. He was the youngest of the three. My father was the oldest, with Aunt Rita in the middle of the three. Granny Ines was their mother.

Uncle Sully had an attitude when it came to me and my father. He often caused drama at family functions. The last was a Sunday dinner where he accused his mother of ignoring his two children in favor of me. It got ugly. Thankfully, I hadn't seen him or his family since then.

"And, he has been super sweet with mama since then. He brings gifts and treats, but she's still mad. She won't completely forgive him until he goes to see Tito."

"Let me guess, he still won't go?"

"Not even an option for him. I expect her not to open the door for him until he does."

"I would believe it."

I haven't seen my father in a while either. I should make that a priority for my next day off. Granny might ban me from the house if I didn't go see him soon. If that happened, Sawyer wouldn't forgive me if he missed out on any of Granny's Sunday dinners.

So, I had to pick either my Granny being upset with me or one of my best friends. I loved them both, so I needed to keep them happy.

We wrapped up lunch, and I drove her home.

"Granny's home. You should come in and say hello."

"Yeah, I think I will."

Walking in the house, we found both Granny Ines and Lolly sitting in the living room visiting over hot tea and cookies.

"Oh, hello, Jessie!" Granny Ines said. "I wasn't expecting to see you."

"I had the day off, so I called Aunt Rita to go to lunch." I smiled. "Hi, Ms. Lolly."

"Hi, darlin', how are you?"

"I'm well. How are you?"

"Honestly, a bit shook up after Donna Overton's death. People knew there was no love lost between us, but I had just spoken to her thirty minutes or so before that. She apologized again for the problem at my Ray's funeral."

"How did she seem when you saw her?"

"Typical Donna, surveying the room, checking out the men." She frowned. "Now she never hit on my Ray, and even if she would have, he would have shut her down."

"Did you notice if she was eating the food I'd brought?"

Granny glared at me. She likely knew I was fishing for the investigation, but I needed answers. I hated waiting for the police to give them to me.

"Honestly, I didn't notice that. We ran into each other in the hallway though, so never saw her actually go in the visitation room."

"Do you want some tea, Jessie?" Granny asked. The firm tone of her voice meant to stop and let the topic change.

"No, thank you, Granny. I should probably get going. I need to stop by the grocery store and then do some chores at the house."

"Are you sure? You only just got here and it has been so long since I just got to visit with you," Lolly said.

Granny gave me the look. That stern look that moms and grandmothers give. I knew she meant for me to be polite and not ask any questions about the murder.

Message received.

"Yeah, I have things to do, but I just wanted to say hi." I walked over, kissing my grandmother and hugging Ms. Lolly and Auntie Rita.

Back in my car, I thought about all the bits of information I had learned today. Auntie Rita had a point that the clue board could come in handy with this. I would make a quick stop at the store for dinner and then fill in the clues that I knew once I got home.

Darcy, Tilly, and, as much as I hated to admit it, maybe Ms. Lolly would be added as a suspect. I didn't have much else to go on and the only motive seemed to be jealousy and possibly adultery. With Ms. Lolly, the motive could be that Donna had ruined her husband's funeral.

That was over a year ago, so I can't imagine she would still be that upset about it. Though she loved her husband very much and I'm sure the added drama on such a day wasn't something you get over or forget easily. She said as much today.

I zipped through the store, grabbing everything I needed to make my friends a good homemade dinner. Tonight's menu was my version of the Marry Me Chicken recipe that was all the rage online. It was good as it was, but I tweaked it by adding bacon and spinach.

Once I had the groceries put away, I checked the time. Plenty before my roommates got home from work, so I could start putting clues on the board.

I wrote it by hand versus printing anything like we did before. I put the three names with the motive under each. Stepping back, I knew it wasn't much to go on, but it was a start.

I decided to add Caruso Funeral Home but no motive under it yet. It would take more digging, but after Gio's weird behavior and the paper invoice, I thought it was worth having at least the name on the board.

As I got more, I could add it.

With that done, I went to make dinner for my friends and just enjoy the rest of my day off.

Chapter Five

Before work, mug of coffee in hand, I stared at the lame clue board with its few names and the motives underneath each. Jealousy and adultery were good enough reasons in the movies and the crime drama shows to kill someone, but was it in reality?

I thought about what Sawyer said about money laundering. Could the funeral home be a front for money laundering? Even though I did have Caruso's on the board, should I add that as a motive?

"What are you doing?" Vee asked, coming in behind me.

She was dressed for work. No matter how many times I saw her dressed up in her postal uniform, I always felt so proud of my friend. She took her job seriously and loved being the face of the postal office. At least, that's what she had said many times over the years.

"Just staring at this stupid thing. I need more clues, but it's been just over a week since the murder." I took a sip of coffee. "I guess more will come."

"Yeah, and they will clear you of all charges soon. I am sure of it."

"Yeah, they better."

Sawyer came down in his uniform, hair a mess, but otherwise, looking quite handsome. He wildly tossed his hair, trying to get it to lay flat. His hair was straight like mine, but sometimes it got out of hand.

"I fell asleep with wet hair." He groaned.

"Well, ya look good." I chuckled. "I made breakfast for y'all. It's in the kitchen."

We all headed into the kitchen where I had made us each an omelet with our favorite fillings. For Sawyer, onions, peppers, and turkey sausage. Vee liked mushroom and spinach. I had a mix of both with turkey sausage, peppers, and mushrooms.

"You outdid yourself on this."

"I love having a best friend who is a chef!"

I smiled at them both. Cooking was my love language. Growing up without a strong sense of security, food was the one thing that gave me comfort. My granny and aunt tried to make me feel secure in their house, but my mother was a mess and would just show up to take me with her, only to return me the next day.

Granny would make a large pot of caldo de pollo or a platter of enchiladas, and it would feel like home. Even with their love and support, I was always worried my mother would come rip me from it.

"I've got cleanup." I said, as we all finished our food.

"You sure?" Sawyer asked.

"Yeah, I still have time before work, but you both need to get going."

Vee looked at the time and made a yep sound, jumping from her seat.

"Thanks!" They said in unison, then waved as they headed out.

I grabbed the empty plates, rinsing them before sticking them in the dishwasher. I added soap then pushed start.

Now it was my turn to check the time.

Score. Plenty of time for another cup of coffee.

I sat at the kitchen island and started scrolling through the various social media feeds. I was happy that I didn't have to rush out. With the restaurant working well, I didn't feel the need to rush. Plus, Noah and I weren't working on a murder investigation together this time, so no reason for me to head in early.

As I was scrolling, a few familiar faces popped up in the feed. It was my little brothers at the beach for a weekend away with my stepdad and our mother.

Gee, thanks family, for the invitation.

Not that I would have gone, but they could have at least thought to ask me. This is how it had been since Bryan and Chris were born. I became the forgotten child.

Regardless of if I wanted to be a part of their lives or not, seeing their smiling faces with waves crashing behind them and sun kissed noses, I felt a little sick to my stomach. I flipped through all the pictures, including one she'd captioned '*Family* Fun', which set off another round of evil butterflies in my stomach.

Tears threatened to spill from my eyes. *Bleep*! She's the parent. I am the child. Shouldn't she want to have a relationship with me?

"This is stupid," I mumbled, wiping my eyes.

I should just go to work.

On the way in, I thought about what the soup of the day would be. I wanted to do something to take my mind off my family and their beachy adventures.

Veggie Beef sounds good. I haven't made that yet at the restaurant. It would be a good change up and would make a good soup of the day.

I headed in and straight to work, pulling out all the veggies and the chuck roast I would break down. I chopped, peeled, and diced. Then mixed and browned, and then cooked everything until it was a perfect soup. Hearty and homey feeling.

Focusing on each step and creating this beautiful soup, cleansing the negative feelings, I felt much better and more relaxed as it bubbled in the large cook pot.

"Morning, Chef!" Arlo said, coming in. He was our maintenance man, keeping the restaurant functioning and all the plumbing working. "It smells so good in here."

He rarely commented on the food, so it must be good.

"Oh, thanks. Soup of the day."

"I'm going to have to get some of that later."

"Arlo, that means a lot to me," I gushed.

A blush formed on his face. He smiled and went to the storage closest to get his supplies. Looked like he grabbed everything to clean the outside windows.

As more employees came in, they all commented on the soup. It really helped me feel even better, and soon I forgot about the pictures and my estranged family.

By the end of the day, I was renewed, and the soup nearly sold out. I made a new batch in the afternoon, so the evening shift would have enough. I also took some to go, so we could have it for dinner tonight. My roommates would love it and after smelling it all day, I wanted to eat some myself.

I said goodbye to my staff at three in the afternoon. My phone rang as I pulled out of the parking lot. It was my Aunt Rita.

"Hi, Aunt Rita," I said.

"Hey, Mija. Are you off work?" Her warm, familiar voice filled the car.

"I am. Just left."

"Oh, good. I had my Bible study today." She giggled. "I talked to Tilly and Darcy about Donna."

"You did? And?"

"Tilly said she hasn't seen or thought much about her since their fight. She has since gotten divorced from her husband for cheating. She found out it wasn't Donna that he was having an affair with."

"Oh, really?" I couldn't hide the shock from my voice. Aunt Rita gets all the good gossip. "Who was it?"

"Her own sister, Margie."

"Wait? As in Margie Holden, my eighth-grade English teacher?"

"That's the one. They ran off to Florida." Aunt Rita sounded so proud of her tale. It didn't help the murder case, but it was juicy.

"Oh, poor Ms. Tilly."

"Yeah, I can't even imagine. They had been having an affair for years. Had Tilly not found out, I wonder if they would have just continued like that forever."

I only knew Tilly from around town and through my aunt. I got the impression she was one of those complainers that often asked to see the manager.

"What about Darcy Whittaker?"

"Well, she had a lot to say on the subject. They apparently ran into each other about a month before at another funeral. While they didn't have a physical fight, there were words exchanged and some pushing."

"Oh, my."

"Yeah. I have heard that isn't the only time. It happens anytime they would get near each other. Edie Baker said that she was at the grocery store when she heard yelling in the meat department. Turns out it was Donna and Darcy. The police got involved in that one."

"Well, okay. Anything else?"

"No, that was all I found out, but I will keep my ears and eyes open for any more information."

"Thanks, Auntie. I love you."

"Love you, too, Jessie."

We hung up just as I pulled to the curb in front of my townhouse. I sat there for a moment, thinking about what she said. It really sounded like Darcy and Donna set each other off, but Tilly sounded like a non-issue now. I would have to update the clue board.

I grabbed the soup and went in, putting the soup in the fridge, Then going to the office to stare at the clues. I took Tilly Franco and moved her to the side. I added a sticky note to her name with an update about her situation.

I didn't want to eliminate her name entirely, but for now, she was considered a less likely suspect.

Next, I added the words *'fight a lot'* to Darcy's name and added the sticky note to her name. It still wasn't much to go on, but it's all I had now.

Sighing, I went to shower and change before my roommates got home.

An hour later, I had made a cast iron pan of cornbread to go with the soup and had the soup warming on the stove.

"Honey, I'm home!" Sawyer's familiar greeting came from the front door.

"Oh, my gosh, what smells so good in here?" Vee scurried to check the pot. Her eyes widened as she saw what was inside. "Is this vegetable beef?"

"It is."

"You know I have a weakness for that." She chuckled. "I'll be right back."

She sprinted upstairs. Sawyer smiled and took off behind her. While they changed, I set the table and served dinner for each person.

Vee was down first.

"I guess we have to wait for him before starting, huh?" She laughed.

"Yes!" he yelled as he jumped down the last of the stairs.

We laughed as he slid into his chair.

They both dug in with enthusiasm and then moaned with pleasure. I chuckled and scooped a large bite.

"Oh, this is better than I could have imagined!" I said.

"It is."

"The best."

"No wonder we sold out so quickly."

We ate in silence after that, at least until we got to seconds.

"So, you want gossip?" I asked.

"Always," Vee said.

"Aunt Rita had her Bible study today." I went on to fill them in on everything I had learned.

"So, Donna didn't have an affair with Tilly's husband?"

"No."

"I can't believe Ms. Holden would be capable of that," Sawyer said, around a bite of cornbread.

"I know. She seemed so … straight-laced."

"Did you write it on the board?" Vee asked, dropping her spoon in her bowl and pushing it back. "That was amazing."

"Thanks, and yes, I did put it on the board."

"We can look at it after dinner."

"Yeah, but I still don't think it is enough." I frowned. "Did y'all hear anything at work?"

"Nothing new."

"Well, I did hear about the Caruso Funeral home," Sawyer said, a slow grin forming on his face.

"What?" Vee and I sat forward.

"Yeah, Steve, he works on the loading dock with me," Sawyer looked at me. I nodded. "He said he used to pick up large shipments from them. They would be shipped to Pinehurst and then a week later, he would deliver boxes that looked and weighed oddly the same back."

"So?"

"So? Are you serious?" He slapped the table with a laugh.

"Yeah, I don't get it."

"Well, oh, I forgot to say he is adding a lot of insurance to them. Like valuing it at over a thousand dollars. Sometimes those packages would go missing."

I stared at Sawyer. I had no idea what he meant. Was I just being dense here?

"You're going to have to connect the dots for her. She doesn't know how the post office works."

"It is how they launder the money that way. One, he is shipping something out and back to himself, likely marking it as some kind of goods. Then he is adding a value to it so that he can then claim the insurance."

"I guess maybe." It felt like he was grasping at straws, but it was worth looking into. "Actually, now that you mention it, I saw him doing something weird when I left there yesterday."

"What?"

"What was he doing?"

"He was looking guilty and loading some large bag into a van."

"Like a body bag?"

"No, not like that. More of a duffle bag, like a gym bag."

"We have to write that on the board."

"I did write Caruso, but I didn't write a motive yet."

"To the board!" Vee yelled, running from the room.

Sawyer winked, "I've got clean up. Go!"

I laughed and followed Vee. She already had money laundering, postal fraud, and weird bag. She stuck that to the paper with Caruso Funeral Home written on it.

"Alright, we are getting somewhere," I said.

"Yes, we are. It is still not enough." She wrapped her arm around me, as we stood there staring at the clues.

"Well, we aren't going to solve this tonight. Ice cream?"

"Ice cream and that new show is coming on."

That was the way we spent the rest of the evening, eating ice cream, watching a new police drama, and trying to force myself not to think about the murder.

Chapter Six

"Chef, guy here to talk to you. Says his name is Max," Jordan said, coming to my station.

"Max? Okay, I'll be right there. Offer him something. Anything he wants."

"Yes, Chef." She turned back to the dining room.

We hadn't spoken in years, except on an occasional bump in here or there, then on the day of the funeral when he came to pick up Donna's body. Why was he seeking me out now? It wasn't like we had been close friends.

Oh, maybe he has some information for me.

"Hannah, can you watch my station?"

"Yes, Chef, no problem."

I washed my hands, checked my reflection.

Good enough.

Then went to see what this reunion was all about.

Stepping out into the dining room, I saw that we had a fairly full house. *Bleep*, this was not a good time for an interruption, but I smiled and walked to where Max was snacking on biscuits and sipping an iced tea.

"Oh, hey, Jess! Long time," he said when he saw me.

"Yeah, hey. Twice in one week, well, a little over a week. That's a record or something." I laughed.

"Well, I come with sort of good news."

"Oh, really?"

"Yeah," he lowered his voice. "The initial autopsy results are in, and it should rule you out as a suspect."

"Really? That would be awesome."

"I won't get too technical on you, but we found signs that lead me to believe it was oleander used to kill her." He looked around. "I can't imagine you would have access to those. Most in this town have been pulled up and destroyed years ago."

"I kind of remember when that was happening."

"Yes, we when we were still in school there was a serial killer using that to kill their victims. It ended up a cold case, but since then it was one of the things our lab always checks for."

"Where does that leave the investigation, then?"

"Honestly, don't know. I gave the information to the police this morning and then came over here. They will have to determine where the plant came from."

I thought about what he said. It would be easy if it was someone in town doing this, because they had pulled up most of the plants years ago. It would be easy to spot one. Though, I can't remember the last time I saw one. I looked at him, realizing that this could get him in hot water.

"Can't you get in trouble for telling me this?"

"Yes, probably," he said with a smile.

"So, why are you telling me? It's not like you owe me or that we've been close friends over the years?"

"Actually, I do owe you." He exhaled sharply. "Remember your fifth birthday party?"

"Vaguely." My life kind of fell apart not long after that.

"Well, I wet my pants and there were so many people, and I was crying and embarrassed. You took my hand, helping me find my mother. You never made fun of me or laughed. You were sweet and caring, and you were only five years old yourself. It was something that I remember still today because it meant so much."

"Oh, wow, I do remember that." Funny the impact we have on others' lives that we don't always remember.

"When I saw your face as we were taking out the body, I imagined that's what I must have looked like to you all those years ago. Scared and lost. That's when I knew I needed to help in any way I could."

"Oh, Max, I don't know what to say." Tears sprung to my eyes.

A small gesture as a child has come back to help me in the present. I'd felt so lonely as a child, especially after my family fell apart, but then in middle school, I met Vee and Sawyer. They had been by my side ever since. Now, as an adult, I am getting help from many of my past classmates. Officer Rafferty, Elias, who owned the local mechanic's shop, and now Max.

Long story on the former two, but here was the latest helper from my past and I didn't know what to say. Thank you seemed so hollow.

"Nothing. Just happy I could give you a little good news, but if the police come talk to you, please act like you didn't already know."

"Of course! Do you have any theories on where it came from?"

"Nah but hoping the police will work that out." He downed the rest of the iced tea. "What do I owe for this?"

"That's on the house." I smiled.

"Really? Are you sure?"

"Of course! You just cleared me of murder, it's the least I can do."

"Ha, well, okay. Thanks!" He stood. "Are you still friends with Vee Paz?"

"Uh, yeah?"

"I had a huge crush on her back in middle school." He stared absently for a second. "Oh well, take care. If you ever need anything, give me a call. Happy to help."

He waved as he made his way out. I waved but didn't really see him. My mind was processing all this new information. Oleander poisoning.

I remember when I was traveling a lot for competitions, I saw them in a few places. But other than that, I never really thought about them.

I couldn't wait to get home to add it to the board. I just needed to finish out my shift first. Since I was out of the kitchen for a minute, I took the opportunity to make the rounds to each of the customers' tables.

"How is everything?" I asked each. The response was overall positive.

"These biscuits are our new favorite thing here!"

"The soup is as good as always."

"Everything is wonderful."

I was a humble person normally, but hearing the praise really stroked my ego. With my pride overflowing, I went back to the kitchen.

Today at three, our slow time here, we would have a quick staff meeting. During the meeting, I was going to pitch the idea of the cornbread contest for the apprentices and the rest of the staff will judge it.

Right at three, we had a book club come in for a late lunch or early dinner. They were giggly and chatty. Ava was the server on duty for that table. I also asked if Keegan, one of my line cooks, would stay behind and start their order.

"I'll fill you both in, and I promise to be quick with the meeting, so you won't be alone long." I smiled. "But if you need support, stop us."

They got to work while I went on with the meeting.

"Just like to do a check in with everyone. How's everything going? What's working? What's not?"

"We keep getting tons of compliments about Parker's biscuits," Jordan said.

There was a round of agreement.

"Anything else before I move on?"

A few grumbles about an unhappy customer and then we had a few supply issues recently, but nothing much. It was them venting mostly, and I was glad they felt comfortable sharing their thoughts with me.

"Alrighty, so now on to the next bit of business, Shayla, Jacoby, Brooklynne, I have a project for the three of you. I will want the rest of the staff to help me with it." I paused for drama. "I want to offer cornbread along with our biscuits, and I want you to come up with a recipe. We will have the staff judge. Winner has their recipe added to the menu."

There were murmurs all around. The apprentices looked stunned, exchanging surprised looks among themselves.

"Really, Chef?" Jacoby asked.

"Really. I think you all have the potential to win," I said. "The jalapeños with the honey flavor just worked. Excellent."

The rest of the staff started offering words of encouragement.

"This is going to be fun!"

"Y'all can do it for sure."

"We are here to help you."

Ava signaled to me. She pointed towards the kitchen.

"Okay, I think that's all I have. We need to go help Keegan and Ava."

Everyone looked around, then hopped up, getting right to work. They worked like a well-oiled machine. I ensured everyone was good before I clocked out. With everything running well, I went to the office to grab my stuff.

Noah was walking out so we walked out together.

"That was a good idea, Jess," Noah said.

"I was eating with Aunt Rita, and she had that idea for us. Well, the idea that we serve cornbread. I came up with the little project."

"I think Duncan would be proud."

Duncan Jones was my culinary arts teacher from high school, and he had served as my mentor. He was still the instructor there. We had recently partnered to hire our three apprentices.

"Oh, I should call him to tell him," I said.

"Yes, you should. I bet he would love to hear about this."

We waved goodbye, and I climbed into my car. When my phone was connected via Bluetooth to the car, I called Mr. Jones.

"Hello?"

"Mr. Jones, it's Jessica Vasquez."

"Jessie! Hi, good to hear from you."

"I wanted to reach out really quick to you. I gave the three students an assignment to come up with a cornbread recipe we could use here in the restaurant."

"Oh, wow, that sounds like a good deal. I support this. I can do a lesson here about it to help them out a bit, but those three are going to come up with some good recipes, I'm sure."

"I knew you would love it, but I wanted to let you know before they come to class tomorrow."

"Thanks! I can't wait to work with them."

We made some small talk for a moment, but then hung up. Tonight, Sawyer had a date with Riley. She was a girl he had been dating for a little over a month now. I didn't exactly like her. She had no filter, just said whatever came to her mind.

With him going out, Vee and I were going to get sushi and watch a movie. Just the girls tonight. It was going to be fun.

Arriving home, I went to shower and change. I stood under the hot water, letting it run down me. It felt good to my sore body, but I had a good day. It was nice.

When I was properly cleaned, I turned off the water and then grabbed a fluffy pink towel to dry myself. Wrapped in the towel, I padded to my bedroom to find clothes. Instead, I found Lulu waiting on the bed. She saw me and started meowing and pacing.

"Did you miss me today?" I scratched her under the chin, then around her ears. She began purring and rubbing against me. "I take that as a yes. You aren't usually this affectionate."

Once she was bored with me, I got myself dressed in one of Colt's Neal Barney shirts. This one was a Yeti with white flowers around it. It was my new favorite shirt to wear around the house.

Lulu and I made our way downstairs, where I headed straight to the office to add the oleander as the next clue. Under it, I added a big question mark. Where had it come from?

On my drive home, I looked around as best I could for any sign of an oleander. There were tons of gardens with perfectly manicured bushes, bright flowers, and large flowering trees. However, I didn't see any oleanders.

As I was standing in front of the board, studying it, the familiar greeting was called out from the front door.

"Honey, I'm home!" Sawyer called out.

"I'm in here!" I yelled.

"Oh, oh, oh! Are we working on the clue board tonight?" Vee giggled and came running. "Oh, you are! A new clue?"

"Yeah, Max Reeder stopped by the restaurant today to give me an update."

"Max Reeder, really?" A blush crept up her face.

Should I tell her he had a crush on her back in the day? No, no, I think he is married now, so no point bringing it up. Plus, it wasn't my business.

"Yeah, he works at the coroner's office," I said. "He told me preliminary autopsy was consistent with oleander poisoning, though there isn't an exact test for it."

"Wow! Like those cases back when we were in school?" Vee said.

"How do you remember this stuff?" Sawyer asked.

"Y'all didn't watch the news?"

We both shook our heads.

"Well, there was someone going around poisoning people. It took place while we were still in middle school and high school and spanned several years. First, it was that guy who was raping all those girls. Then it was the mother who drowned her two small children and then a hit and run driver that killed ... oh what was her name? Science teacher?" Vee said.

"Ms. McCallister?"

"Yes! That's it."

"Oh, geez! That's a lot of ... violence," I said.

"Yeah, there were a few others. The media nicknamed them the Morality Killer. Awful name, but honestly, it fits. It was like they were trying to right all the wrongs. Once the police figured out they were using the oleanders, the police suggested they be destroyed. It was a long process, not overnight. The city council did several studies then they added it to the ballot. The town voted, and well, obviously, it all passed. Now they are no longer allowed in town."

"Now that you mention it, I do vaguely remember that," Sawyer said. "My mom had a few, and she was so mad to have to pull them up, but in the end, she got crepe myrtles and liked them better."

"Yeah, I think they are beautiful, too," I said. "But what Max said is that the case went cold?"

Vee nodded her head. "Yes, that's what I remember, too. There were a few random cases after that, but not with oleanders. I think one person died from insulin overdose and another from fentanyl. No idea if they are related, but they were the same types of killings."

"Our police department doesn't have a good track record, do they?" I crossed my arms. "So, now what? We just let this go? Assume this was just a repeat of this Morality Killer because everyone hated Donna?"

"Could be the motive, but not a very good one," Vee said.

"You really think Ms. Lolly killed Donna?" Sawyer pointed to her name on the board.

"No, not really, but I don't have much yet, and she did have a significant run in with Donna at her husband's funeral."

"I was there. It was pretty epic." Vee chuckled. "But you could argue that, if it was Ms. Lolly, she could have reason to kill Tilly Franco, too. Tilly is the one who came there looking for a fight with Donna."

"Um, that's true." I stared at the board.

Bleep, I hated having these question marks on people who I'd known most of my life. Lolly was a good friend of my grandmother.

She and her husband, Ray, had always given me a safe place and fun childhood memories.

I couldn't even wrap my head around looking at her as a suspect. How could I? Granny would never forgive me.

"Well, I wish I could stay and solve crimes, but I am off to change and then gotta pick up Riley." He kissed our foreheads, then jogged upstairs.

"I'll go change, then we can order food," Vee said. "Girl's night! Whoop, whoop!"

She danced out of the room. I really had to think about what she said, but for now, I was going to settle in for girls' night with sushi, gossip, and a movie, and try really hard to put this out of my mind.

Chapter Seven

I was plating a shrimp and grits order for the tenth time today. It had become a popular item. I had to be honest; it was a favorite of mine, too.

"Order up. Shrimp and grits."

Marco, who was normally a busser, came forward. We had to shift people today due to illness.

"Got it, Chef. Table 15," he said, as he gathered the rest of their order from the window and took it out.

I wiped down my station and looked around my kitchen and staff. This was my favorite place to be. I didn't have to think about anything but cooking. This place made sense when things in the outside world didn't always.

Shayla came in the back door with a huge smile on her face. She rarely smiled like this, except when she was creating something delicious.

"Good afternoon, Chef! I brought cornbread to be sampled."

Bingo. I was right.

"Oh, nice! Let's set it up over on this empty station." I gestured her to our one empty spot. Jacoby and Brooklynne should be bringing theirs today, too. "This smells amazing!"

Shayla beamed with pride. "I worked really hard on this."

"It looks like it. Once Jacoby and Brooklynne arrive with theirs, we'll start the contest."

"Thanks. I'll go wash up and get on the line with Natalie."

"Great." I smiled after her. I watched her wash up and join Natalie. Shayla had a wonderful energy today. That warmed my heart.

Within a few minutes, the other two arrived, as did Parker, so he took over as head chef for the night. I grabbed some sticky notes and a bowl, then set them next to each cornbread. Since it was a blind taste test, I labeled them as A, B, and C and didn't tell anyone else who the baker of each was.

I knew which was which, but it didn't stop me from cutting a small square of each. They were all amazing. It was going to be a difficult choice.

The staff started coming over to taste the sweet and savory cornbread.

"Oh, my gosh, this one is good."

"But wait until you try this one!"

"It has to be this one."

"No, this one!"

I watched for a few minutes before heading to the office.

"Cornbread is served. Y'all might want to get in there before everyone else eats it all," I said to Noah and Cullen.

"Oh, I'm on it!" Cullen jumped up, running out.

"I'm not a big fan of cornbread. I'll let the others have it," Noah said.

"You are missing out. They are all good."

"Again, not a fan, but glad that they did good. I am still cheering for them all." He smiled.

"Hey, Chef. Some lady is here for you. Says her name is Lolly," Jordan said with a shrug.

"Oh, tell her I'll be right there. Offer her whatever she likes."

"She already ate but wanted to say hi before she leaves," Jordan said.

"Ah, okay. I'm coming." I looked at Noah and then followed Jordan to the dining room.

She pointed to a booth near the front. Lolly was chatting with Skye, her server. Skye was smiling, but I'm sure she was hoping to go home. It was the end of her shift, but I knew she would be polite and friendly as long as it took.

"Hi, Lolly, Thanks, Skye. See you tomorrow." I turned to her, giving her a wink.

"Thanks, Chef." She smiled in relief.

I took a seat. "How are you?"

"I'm wonderful. I had your alphabet soup and a turkey club. It was all excellent."

"I love to hear that. It is good to see you again."

"I told you I would stop by and here I am. I had been meaning to come in, but you know, just busy with volunteering and Bible study. Then I visited with Diane. You remember my daughter, right?"

"Of course. How is she?"

"She is doing well. Working, happy."

"Her kids are in college, right?"

"Yes, both boys are. Jack is at Harvard Law and James is Cornell."

"That's amazing. Good for them."

"I just hate that Ray isn't here to see them. Those two boys were the apple of his eye, you know."

"I remember."

Mr. Ray was always bragging about his grandsons.

"They're both so smart. They are going to do something big, huge. Maybe save this world," he would boast. "And don't get me started on how good they are at sports. They get that from me. I used to play baseball back in my day."

He would then go off reminiscing about this game or that.

"He would be so proud of the young men they are now." She got a faraway look. "Oh, sorry, dear. I seem to be doing that more and more. Going off into my own head."

"It's okay. I get it."

"You'll see when you are my age." She chuckled.

"I'm sure." I had no idea what to say to that. But I heard the phrase often from my granny's friends. She had offered information about her daughter and grandsons, but not her son. "So how is Alex doing?"

"Oh, he is good. Working in Virigina right now. Keeping busy." She grimaced but didn't elaborate further. Her expression told me to let it go.

"Well, nice." I didn't want to pry if she wasn't going to share more.

"Shame about Donna Overton. They said you found her body. That must have been awful."

My throat went dry at her words. Every time I thought about finding Donna, it was jarring.

"Oh, um, yeah, very sad, and it was an awful ... thing to find."

"I know people think I didn't like her for crashing Ray's funeral, and yes, I was upset, but I never wished her ill. She was actually a nice person, and I didn't believe all those rumors about her flirting. She was amazing to me with planning Ray's funeral. Always asking about how I was, checking on me." She choked slightly. "She even worked tirelessly to try to find Ray's jewelry when it went missing."

"What jewelry?"

"He had been wearing his wedding ring, a Rolex, and a gold chain with a cross. When I looked in the casket at the service, they were gone."

"Really? Did you ever find them?"

"No. The police were no help. Donna was the only one who really tried to find them. Gio Caruso only cares about money." She made a spitting sound. "I curse him! His whole family!"

I was taken aback by her outrage. She was not an angry woman normally. I have never once heard her even raise her voice.

With no idea how to reply, I simply offered a weak smile and a nod.

"Oh, I'm sorry. I shouldn't unload all my troubles on you. I just wanted to tell you I enjoyed your food. This place looks wonderful." She looked around. "I love the local art you added. One thing our town does well, art."

I looked around, trying to see it through different eyes. Eyes that weren't the ones that carefully picked each item to create a cozy atmosphere and capture the feeling of the town.

"It does," I agreed.

"Ray used to love the arts. He often painted."

"I remember. I loved watching him."

She smiled at me. "He loved having you at our house. Well, I'm all settled here. I will see you again soon. I have a feeling that I will be a regular now."

"Oh, next time let me know before you pay. It will be on the house."

"No, dear, you won't make money giving food away. I am happy to pay my fair share." She hugged me and then made her way out, waving to all the servers and the hosts as she passed them.

I went back to the kitchen to check on the cornbread. It was nearly gone.

"Wow, this is going quick," I said to the students as I walked by. They grinned, sharing a look between them. I could tell they were proud. "Mr. Jones will be so proud."

As I drove home later, I thought about Ms. Lolly. She was surprisingly upset with Gio Caruso and rightly so if Ray's jewelry had been so carelessly lost like that, or worse, stolen. I didn't know much about how that worked, but assumed they would keep the body secure until the viewing and service.

A thought popped into my head.

Maybe I should add Gio to the suspect list. Not just the funeral home itself, but actually Gio. I would add missing jewelry, too, even if it was four years ago.

Rushing in the door, I headed straight to the office, grabbing two pieces of paper. On one, I wrote Gio and missing jewelry on the other, then pinned them on the board. The missing jewelry, I put on the paper for the funeral home. I couldn't pin it on Gio just yet, but I just had a feeling that he was involved in something, even if it wasn't directly related to Donna's death.

"No idea if this means anything, but it is worth a shot," I said out loud. I looked at the other names and clues on the board. "I would be so embarrassed if anyone knew about this."

Meaning the people on the suspect list, but Granny likely wouldn't like it much either, especially with her good friend's name on it.

Exhaling sharply, I turned to go shower and change. I wasn't going to solve this today.

An hour later, I was cooking spaghetti and meatballs for my roommates, when they came laughing and singing. Clearly, they'd had a good day.

"Oh, spaghetti and meatballs! You read my mind," Sawyer yelled. "Do we have enough for me to invite Riley?"

I fought the urge to groan but turned with a smile. "Yeah, of course. You know I cook for a small army."

"You're the best!" He kissed my cheek and then ran upstairs to change.

"You're a good sport about her," Vee said, taking a seat at the kitchen island.

"Well, just because she is blunt, doesn't mean that she did anything to me, exactly."

We hadn't seen eye to eye when I was investigating Colt's murder a few months ago. She had been rude and more than once came to my restaurant because Sawyer had broken up with her. She'd wanted my help in getting him back. Each time she would leave, something had happened to my car. The last one being an explosion. I loved that car.

She was cleared and apologized for being rude. I believed that she didn't have anything to do with the attacks on me, but I didn't like how blunt she was with her thoughts. I really hoped she reined that in. This would be the first time I would see her in about a month.

"So, how was your day?"

"It was good. The apprentices brought in their cornbread for the staff to judge. They were all amazing."

"That's fun."

"Oh, and Lolly came by the restaurant today. We had an interesting conversation."

"Interesting how?" She sat forward.

"Interesting in that she seemed fine with Donna, but cursed Gio Caruso's name. Said that Ray's jewelry went missing before his service."

"Oh, oh! I remember this. She was so upset that day. I had never seen her angry before, but that day she was a little ball of rage. Donna was running all over, searching for the items. Gio was not moved at all. He just said they couldn't be liable for lost items. It was the risk of having expensive jewelry on the body."

"Wow, that's not very ... sympathetic." But I suppose there is that risk. Still, he could have shown some emotion or empathy towards her.

"Lolly said that she had been assured the body would be secured until just before the service, and she said she arrived as they opened his coffin. It was missing at that point."

"So, it could have been an employee?"

"Yes! And I don't know if you remember, but there have been a lot of missing items from there. But Gio always says the same. It is the family's risk."

"I can understand that to a point, but there should be some reasonable expectation of safety, too. People are trusting them at a low point, a sad point in their lives."

"I agree." She stood. "Oh, I better go get ready for our company."

I turned back to the stove, plastering a smile on my face as I mentally prepared for the Riley storm to come.

About fifteen minutes later, dinner was finished, and there was a knock at the door.

"I got it!" Sawyer flew down the stairs. "Hey, come in."

"Thanks, babe!" She leaned up to kiss him, then saw me. "Oh, hey, Jess. How are you?"

"I'm good. How are you?"

"I'm good, too. Thank you for having me for dinner." She smiled sweetly.

"Well, it's ready," I said. "I'll just go check on Vee."

I started up the stairs when I heard Riley ask Sawyer about the board. I stopped to listen.

"It looks like y'all are doing another investigation. Who this time?"

"Oh, um, Donna Overton at Caruso's Funeral Home."

"Nobody liked her, so why put in that effort? From what I hear, no big loss."

"Do you really think that?" he asked.

"No, I mean, I just … Why do you guys do this? Why not leave it to the police? Look what happened to Jess last time and there was that guy who shot into your house. Isn't that stuff scary?"

Vee's door opening broke my focus, so I missed the rest of their conversation. I jogged up the last few steps.

"Hey, was just coming to get you. Dinner is ready." But then I pointed her back to her room. Once we were inside her room, I lowered my voice. "They are in the office talking about the board."

"What were they saying?"

"She was asking about why we didn't leave it to the police and why would I keep doing this when I got hurt last time?"

"Well, she has a point."

"I know she has a point, but … Okay, Earl was my friend. Colt was my friend. Donna isn't anyone to me. I barely even knew her name before Lois's funeral. But since they were saying she was poisoned, it became personal. I don't feed poisoned food." I tried to keep my voice low, so Riley couldn't hear me. I didn't want to start a fight or hurt her feelings, but I just wanted to vent my frustrations.

"Yeah, I get it. These are personal to you. Riley doesn't know that, and we know she is blunt so…" She shrugged.

"Yeah, you're right. Let it go, Jess. Let it go." I frowned. "I just want to ensure that people know I didn't poison anyone with my food. Even if Max did confirm it couldn't have been my food, I just want to make sure. I'm ahead of where I thought I'd be at this point with my business. The restaurant is making more profit than I expected at this point. It is beyond my wildest dreams. I mean, I'm not making enough yet to say I'm rich or even to do anything crazy, but it is above what I had planned for or thought possible at this point."

"That is amazing, but you have a great concept and excellent food."

"I think people expected me to stick with my roots, but we have different types of Latin foods already. Nobody was doing much Southern foods."

"Well, your Hispanic spin on those Southern classics makes it uniquely yours." She smiled. "Wait? Didn't you say dinner was ready?"

"Oh, bleep, yes, let's go eat!"

Riley was on her best behavior through dinner. She didn't mention the board, Donna, or anything related to past investigations. Then after dinner, they played video games while Vee and I just watched and played on our phones. A fairly typical evening for us, but with a guest.

Chapter Eight

"Hey, I was doing some digging into Caruso's and missing jewelry and items," Vee said over breakfast the next morning. "There have been dozens of cases over the past six years."

She thrust her phone at me. There was an article from last year about a couple whose daughter had been in a bad accident just weeks before her college graduation and passed away. They wanted to bury her with her class ring and a special locket they had planned to give her for a graduation gift.

It was put on her the night before; the casket was closed and then when it was opened in front of them the next morning; the items were gone.

"That had to be an inside job, right?" I asked Vee, as if she would know, but we could speculate together.

"Yes, has to be!"

"You think this is related to Donna's death?"

"Honestly, yes. I mean, what if someone was trying to … I don't know, keep her quiet or maybe get revenge?"

"Wow." I handed her the phone back and thought about that for a moment. "Just like the Morality Killer."

"Yes, my thoughts exactly."

It was crazy. I was thinking this was simpler than it was. Someone with access to the rare-in-this-area oleander had done it. Shouldn't be hard to find who had those, but now it was looking like some kind of theft and possibly revenge.

"Do you think this is drug related stuff or maybe mob related?" I asked her.

"Maybe. Like a drug ring type thing?"

"Yeah, where they steal to fund their business or habit or whatever. I don't even know how that works."

"Me neither, but this is getting exciting!" She squealed.

"What are we squealing about this early?" Sawyer said, yawning his way into the kitchen.

"What if Donna's murder was related to a drug ring?" Vee said, way too excited.

"That sounds dangerous, honestly. Not something I think I would squeal about."

"You're such a downer." She stuck her tongue out.

"And you're five." He stuck his tongue out.

"You are both children." I laughed. "What do I do with this new information?"

"On the board!" Vee yelled, jumping up from the stool and running to the office.

I looked over at Sawyer, who rolled his eyes, but then followed her. I grabbed my coffee and did the same. We walked in just as she was pinning the words 'drug ring' with a question mark to the board.

I took in all the things on it. This was more than I had at first with Colt's murder, and we didn't have this with Earl's murder. It could have come in handy, and maybe I wouldn't have missed so many signs. Thinking back on Earls', the clues seemed so obvious to me now.

"Are we getting better at this or are there just more clues?"

"Maybe both," Vee said.

We stood there quietly, Sawyer and I sipping coffee. Vee flitting back and forth, looking at different angles, and then hemming and hawing. She was visibly processing the information.

"What is Granny Ines making for Sunday dinner?" Sawyer finally asked.

"I think her tacos al pastor and stuffed peppers."

"Oh, yummy. I can't wait."

My phone buzzed. It was Detective Upton. I hadn't talked to him in a week or so, not since the day of Donna's murder.

"Well, whatever he wants, I hope it doesn't put a wrinkle on Sunday dinner." I walked to the other room. "Hello, Detective."

"Hey, Jess. Do you have a moment?"

"I do."

"Great. So, I received the initial results back."

"On a Sunday?"

"No, um, but I had to follow up and then life and just now getting back to you."

"And I hope you have good news for me."

"I have a feeling you already know, but yes, this information clears you."

"As I knew it would but thank you for telling me. I don't suppose you could give me additional information?"

"You know that I can't, but I tell you what I can."

"Which I appreciate." I paused. "Um, unrelated, but have you heard of the thefts at Caruso's Funeral Home?"

"Thefts?"

"I read about a family who discovered that a class ring and locket were missing from their daughter's coffin. There have been other cases like this, but this one is the most recent."

"Yes, I am the investigator on those cases."

"Oh, I thought you did just homicide."

"We are a small department, so I do anything that requires investigating, and what I can't handle. We work with Pinehurst on. They obviously have more resources, and we have an agreement with them."

"Makes sense." I knew I was going to be pushing my luck with my next question, but I blurted it out before I chickened out. "Do you think it is related to Donna's murder?"

I could hear him inhale, then exhale slowly, but wasn't sure if that meant he hadn't yet made that connection or he thought I knew too much.

"As I've said, I can't discuss cases with you." A little voice in the background yelled, "Daddy!"

"Is that Aiden?"

I had met his young son a few times. He was a cute kid, even if I wasn't a huge fan of children. If there was a kid to push me into being a fan, it would be Aiden Upton. He was a sweet, quiet little boy, at least most of the time.

"It is. He wants to go play outside ... I'm coming, buddy ... Jess, sorry, I need to go, but just wanted you to know you are clear."

"Thanks."

"And please stay out of this. Now that you are cleared, you have no personal connection any longer. Okay?"

He hadn't known me for long, but obviously I was easy to read.

"Okay."

It wasn't a promise, but an agreement that I had no intention of keeping. I found her body. I live in this town, and one of the primary suspects, at least on my list, was a close friend of our family. It was very personal to me, whether or not he saw that.

We hung up, and I turned to find my friends staring at me.

"He said I was cleared of the murder, which we knew, but it is now official."

"Well, that's good news, right?" Vee asked.

"Yeah, I guess, but it still feels undone."

"Because it is," she said.

"And we are going to solve it?" Sawyer asked.

I looked at them both. I knew from past experience this could get messy. This could get dangerous, but dang it, I wanted to know what happened and if it was meant to frame me or if that was just a coincidence, I needed to know.

"Yes, we are," I said, proudly.

"So, what's the next step?" Sawer asked.

"I am going to get dressed for our hike. I think better on the trail." I gulped down the last of my coffee and took the mug to the kitchen.

An hour later, we were starting down the longer trail at Milton County Park. It was a perfect day. Low humidity, which was a bonus here where it was always boiling when it was humid. The skies were clear and sunny. Thankfully, it was still early enough in the day that it wasn't too hot. That would come soon enough.

Walking along with my two best friends, I took in the trees, the sounds of the birds, and the warmth of the sun. I loved that I had more time off now. I had two full days off each week, plus my evenings.

A far cry from just a few months ago. It was anywhere from twelve to sixteen-hour days leading up to and then, for the first month or two once we were open.

Now, we were back to hiking a few times a month and then going to Sunday dinners at my grandmother's at least twice a month. We had to coordinate with my Uncle Sully and his family, because we did not mix well. Anytime we were there together, there was some drama and fight. But they were out of town for a family vacation. Though I didn't know where. I rarely paid attention to them.

Same with my own mother. She had remarried and had two sons, my half-brothers. She doted on them as if they were the future kings of the world. It was disgusting, and after she basically threw me away when I was five, I couldn't forgive her.

The only family I had any relationship with were my Granny Ines and Auntie Rita. They live together and once upon a time I lived with them too. They were the only stable thing in my life. Well, aside from Sawyer and Vee.

"Oh, look, a deer," Vee whispered.

Ahead of us on the trail was a deer. She looked our way, then back over her shoulder. We stood as still as possible. A moment passed before two small deer came to stand by her. They twitched their ears and noses our way, before all three darted into the trees and out of sight.

"That was beautiful," Vee said. "I love nature."

"Me too. Its calming for the soul," I said.

We walked on for a few more minutes before we paused at our favorite spot overlooking the lake. We stood there watching the various water birds. This was the most beautiful spot.

Vee wrapped her arms around us both.

"Y'all are my best friends."

"Aw, you're sweet." I squeezed her.

"I love you, silly goof." Sawyer chuckled.

"Why? Because I tell you how I feel?"

"Yeah, but it's sweet."

We stood watching the various waterfowl for a few minutes. A large heron caught a fish. A few ducks paddled along the water. A fish jumped, splashing loudly into the water. There was a soft breeze blowing through the trees.

I inhaled and exhaled slowly several times, enjoying the moment.

"Well, y'all ready to finish up?" I asked.

"Yep, let's go."

We started around again, but as we were halfway to the end, there was a strange noise off the path to our left. We paused, trying to hear.

"What is that?" Sawyer asked, looking in that direction.

"No idea."

"Was it a gunshot?"

"I hear ... like chopping? Like with an axe, maybe?" Sawyer said.

"Yeah, that's what I hear. First a gun shot or shots maybe, then a weird rhythmic sound." I listened closer. "Or is that digging?"

"Yeah, maybe that's what it is." Sawyer said, trying to listen.

"We should go," Vee said. She started speed walking out of the area and straight towards the end of the trail. Sawyer and I hesitated only a minute before we were on her heels.

Back at the car, we noticed two dark sedans in the parking lot. One looked oddly familiar, but I couldn't think of where I'd seen it. It was someone we knew.

Darn, it is on the tip of my tongue. I thought.

"Is that Dimitri Caruso's car?" Vee asked, as if reading my mind.

"That's who I was trying to place. It does look like his car," I said.

"I didn't take him for a hiker," Sawyer added.

Vee and I agreed.

"I don't like this. Let's just get out of here," Sawyer said, pushing the unlock button on his car.

We climbed in and took off before we saw or heard anything else. Whatever was happening in the woods, we didn't need to be involved in it.

Once on the road and away from the park, we all let out a nervous burst of laughter.

"What were we saying earlier about solving a murder?" I asked.

"Right? We run at the first suspicious sound?" Vee laughed.

"I think it was the smart thing for us to do."

"Right? I am not prepared for superhero work today." I laughed.

We drove on quietly, except for the low music on the radio. Growing up in the rougher part of town, we knew what gunshots sounded like and that definitely sounded like two or maybe three. It had echoed off the trees, so it had been hard to know for sure.

However, it was the following sounds that had seemed strange. Was it digging? Was it chopping? Hard to say.

Normally, I would say those sounded very different, but it was at a distance, and it was muffled through the woods. Whatever it was, we didn't have the proper training, experience, or reason to go check it out further.

The cars had me perplexed. Dimitri was a sculptor, an artist. What was he doing out here? Was he working as an enforcer for his father? That is if Gio was doing something criminal. That was just an assumption, a guess based on all the things we had read and things we'd seen.

"Do we think Caruso's is corrupt?" Vee asked.

"Oh yeah, for sure," Sawyer said without hesitation.

"Yes, remember when I said I saw him loading that bag into the van. It had to be something, right?"

"It could have been a body," Vee said.

"It wasn't big enough." I chuckled.

"Or laundered money," Sawyer commented.

"Or a body with money," Vee added.

"Y'all! Really? It wasn't big enough for a body."

"It could have been stolen jewelry." Vee grinned. "That would explain a lot."

The car fell silent as I think the realization hit all of us. The Carusos were doing something nefarious, and it all pointed to stolen jewelry from the coffins.

Bleep. I thought.

"We might need to go poking around at Caruso's," I said flatly.

"Yeah," Both of my friends said.

Chapter Nine

After hiking, we headed back to the townhouse to get ready for Sunday dinner. I was looking forward to seeing Granny and Auntie Rita. While I had seen my aunt recently, I hadn't seen as much of my grandmother. Just a few minutes when I dropped Aunt Rita off.

I showered and dressed in a plain black t-shirt with a gray chunky cardigan sweater. I loved it because it was soft.

"Okay, Lulu, you good for the evening?"

She pawed the water faucet.

"No, you've had enough water."

She meowed, disagreeing with me. I sighed and turned it back on for her.

"Sometimes you are such a diva." I pet her as she gouged herself on water. She was so funny sometimes.

When she'd finally had enough, she looked at me before jumping to the floor and running off to find a nap spot. I laughed, watching her go. I loved that crazy cat.

As I started to head down, I heard a slight curse from Vee's room.

"Vee, you okay?" I knocked at her door.

"My hair ... again," she called from her bathroom.

"Want my help?" I walked in to find her with a flat iron running through her hair, but when she pulled it through, her hair just frizzed up. "Did you use that product I got you?"

"Oh, shoot, no." She fumbled around, looking for it. In the process, she knocked over this bottle or that one.

"I don't know how you live like this. Fifty million products on your counter, but you can never find the one you need." I grabbed the right one and started running it through her hair. Then I grabbed the flat iron and worked it from root to tip, slowly. "Ah, there you are."

"You are magic." She stared at the straight patch of hair I still held between two fingers.

"Not magic. I told you this product is magic."

I continued working at her hair until it was all smooth and silky. She smiled at me in the mirror.

"What would I do without you?"

"Walk around looking like a hot mess," I teased.

"Yeah, probably."

We headed downstairs to find Sawyer playing his game. He looked up, smiling at us when we came down.

"Vee, your hair looks great. I'm assuming Jess helped."

"She did. My hair hero." She giggled.

"Are we ready to go?"

"Yep."

We drove across town singing and chatting. I loved this time with my friends and heading to see my family. What a wonderful day off.

As we drove down the street towards Granny's house, I saw that there were several cars in the driveway and in front of the house.

"Oh, their Bible study group must still be meeting."

"I thought they did that during the week."

"And are in separate groups."

"Yeah, but once a month, they do a larger group together," I said. "Must be today."

There was no other reason for there to be that many cars in front of their house. Not that it was a lot. I counted to five.

Sawyer managed to park across the street in front of the Ramos's house. Mr. Ramos was in his yard weeding when we got out.

"Hi, kids. Sunday dinner?" he yelled.

"Yes, sir."

"Rita dropped us off a couple of plates earlier. It smells amazing. I can't wait for dinner time." He smiled.

"Nice. Enjoy," I said.

He waved as we crossed the street. I opened the door to hear several ladies' voices all mingling together.

"Hello," I called out.

"Jessie!"

"Jess."

"Oh, sweet, Jessica's here."

All the ladies came around from the kitchen. I knew some of the faces, but not everyone. Those we knew greeted the three of us with hugs and a few greeted us with kisses.

Granny came over and wrapped her arms around me. I knew she missed me as much as I had missed her. Even though she was sometimes tough on me, she loved me so very much.

"Does everyone know my granddaughter, Jessica?" Granny asked the group.

Most nodded, like Lolly, Edie, Tilly Franco, and Darcy Whittaker, but a few ladies said no. They are the ones I hadn't met before.

"Oh, wait? You are the chef and owner of The Crock Pot restaurant, right?" one lady said.

"Yes, that's me."

"We love your restaurant. My husband and I go there every Tuesday for lunch. We love the alphabet soup."

"Oh, I love the alphabet soup," Tilly Franco said.

"Me too," Edie added. She had been best friends with Aunt Rita since elementary school. I had known her my entire life.

"Those new biscuits are amazing," another lady said.

"Well, thank you all. That means a lot." I smiled.

"And these are her best friends, Sawyer and Vee." Granny gestured to them.

That introduction was followed by another round of greetings from the ladies.

"It's so good to see you three kids," Ms. Lolly said. "I am happy you all stayed friends over the years."

"Thank you," Sawyer said, hugging her. Lolly's smile brightened.

"I sometimes get to see Vee at the post office," Lolly said. "You're the sweetest. I walk right back out if you aren't at the desk."

"Aw, Ms. Lolly, you're sweet, but all the workers are good."

"Not as good as you." She winked.

"You work there too, right, Sawyer?" Edie asked.

"That's right, Ms. Edie, but I work in the back."

"You have such a handsome smile. We would love to see you at the desk." Lolly flirted.

"Aw, Ms. Lolly, that wouldn't be fair to all the men out there." He winked.

She blushed and giggled.

"Jessie, we heard about the drama with your catering event," Tilly said.

"Oh, um, yeah. Such a shame about Donna Overton," I said.

Darcy snorted, mumbling, "ha, good riddance."

Several ladies gasped at her mockery. A couple laughed quietly.

"Darcy, we all know how you feel," Tilly snickered. "I once felt the same but turns out I might have been barking up the wrong tree."

"Yeah, sorry, Tilly. Perry's loss." Darcy reached for her hand. "But you know that Donna pushed all my buttons. I swear she did it on purpose."

"She flirted with my Edgar during our son's funeral," one lady said. I think her name is Joyce.

"I heard she was sleeping with Gio," another said.

"And Dimitri."

"The son!"

"That's what I heard." Joyce shrugged.

"I wouldn't put it past her."

"She was always causing a scene," another scoffed.

"Ladies, we shouldn't speak ill of the dead," Granny said with click of her tongue. She had done that to me so many times growing up, that I'd lost count. "We should simply pray for her soul."

"You're so right, Ines," Lolly said. "I didn't like that woman, but she is gone and now will face the *ultimate* judgment."

Her tone caused everyone to look at her. She shrugged.

"You all know I'm right." Lolly flashed a sweet, innocent grin. "Sure, she had been sweet to me when my Ray's jewelry had gone missing, and yes, we had found some common ground. It doesn't change the fact that she caused so many problems."

There was silence. A few of the ladies exchanged smirks. Obviously, they were thinking the same as Ms. Lolly. No loss.

"Well, thank you, Ines and Rita. As always, you were wonderful hostesses," Lolly said, grabbing her purse and a small plastic food container. "Thanks for the dinner. I will enjoy this in front of the television later."

"Yes, I guess we better get going, ladies," Edie said. She hugged Rita, then came over to hug me.

"It's so good to see you, Jessie. I plan to come out to The Crock Pot soon. I have heard such good things about it."

She had been out of town for a few months, helping her son and daughter-in-law with their new baby. It was her first grandbaby, and she had been so excited before heading out there months ago.

Her daughter-in-law had a rough pregnancy and labor and needed extra help. Edie was retired, so she had the time to spare. It had worked out for all of them.

"Yeah, it has been going well. Let me know if you come out."

We all walked out onto the small porch to say goodbye and wave. Sawyer walked Ms. Lolly to her car, helping her in.

"You are such a sweet boy. We need more people like you in the world." She patted his face, then shut the door, driving away with a jerky start.

Vee and I exchanged a look. Lolly should probably not be driving any longer, but I wasn't going to tell her. That was something one of her children, Diane and Alex, would need to do. But seeing a neither of them lived close by, they likely didn't even know.

Once all the ladies had left, we all went inside.

"Do you need help cleaning up before dinner?" Vee offered.

"Oh, that would be wonderful," Granny said with a smile.

"We will handle cleanup, you two sit," Sawyer said, grabbing a few teacups.

"Lolly is right, you are the sweetest guy," Auntie Rita said, taking a seat on the couch.

"Yes, thank you," Granny said, sitting in her favorite chair, stretching her feet out across her patchwork ottoman.

The three of us made quick work of the teacups and dessert plates. We then joined Granny and Aunt Rita in the living room.

"Oh, Mija, I talked to your father today," Granny said.

"How is he?"

"He sounds good. Misses you." She paused to give me a stern look. The kind only grandmothers could give. "When are you going to visit him?"

Here comes the guilt trip.

"I was thinking maybe on my next day off."

"That's Wednesday, correct?"

"Yes, ma'am."

"Okay, I'll go with you." She smiled and sat back.

I guess I was stuck going now. I always hated going out to that place. It was a two-to-two-and-a-half-hour drive to that sad, depressing concrete prison where I couldn't even hug my dad, except at the start and end of the visit. Otherwise, we couldn't touch.

He always acted like everything was normal, like he wasn't serving a life sentence for murdering a man. It felt so fake.

Though a few months ago, I realized why he had killed Mr. Jackson. It was in protection of me. My heart broke a little when I realized I had been punishing him for not being there for me and breaking up our family, when all he was doing was taking care of me.

Still, he could have made a different choice. He could have been there for me and for my mom. Then our family would still be together.

I shook that sad thought away and focused on the conversation around me. They were talking about random town news and gossip. Then on to the quarterly art festival that was happening soon, so we talked about that.

"Have you decided if you will have a food booth one day?" Aunt Rita asked.

"I don't know. I am thinking next year, maybe first quarter."

"What would you serve?" Vee asked, excitedly.

"I guess my alphabet soup, Parker's biscuits, and maybe … I don't know."

"June's pimento cheese," Sawyer blurted.

"Maybe so. It is popular." I chuckled. "But I was thinking perhaps some sandwiches or something easy to eat while walking. Soup would be in a bowl with a spoon."

"That would be yummy," Vee said.

"You would be a hit," Aunt Rita added with a smile.

"Well, are you kids ready to eat?" Granny asked.

"Yes, ma'am!" Sawyer said, popping up. "Do you need help with anything?"

"That would be wonderful."

A couple of hours later, with dinner eaten and the kitchen cleaned, we prepared to leave.

"Thank you for dinner. It was delicious, as always," Vee said, hugging both Granny and Aunt Rita.

"Yes, it was excellent," Sawyer said, patting the to-go containers Granny had loaded up for him.

"We are so glad you all enjoyed it." Granny smiled. "And Jessie, come pick me up at eight on Wednesday morning."

"I will be here." I hugged her.

We climbed in the car, waving as we pulled away from the curb.

"Oh, my gosh! That was a crazy afternoon," Vee blurted once we were down the street. "Lolly and Darcy both had strong opinions about Donna."

"Yes, oh my gosh." I turned to face her. "All the ladies had an opinion, but those two, oh boy."

"We should add a few notes to their names on the board."

"Definitely," Sawyer said.

We pulled to the curb in front of our townhouse.

"What is on our doorstep?" Vee pointed.

"Is that a plant?" Sawyer asked.

"Looks like it."

We climbed out and went to look at the plant.

"Is that an oleander?"

"Yeah," Vee said. "Is this some kind of threat?"

"I'm calling the police." I dialed 9-1-1 on my phone.

Ten minutes later, a police cruiser pulled to the curb in front of our townhouse. The lanky frame of our old classmate stepped out of the driver's seat.

"Jess, Jess, Jess," Rafferty's deep voice called. "What trouble have you found now?"

"Hey, Raff. This." I pointed to the plant.

"It's a plant."

"Yeah, obviously, but it's an oleander. The same type of plant that was used to kill Donna Overton."

"Well, dang, alrighty." He pulled out his phone to take pictures. "Was there a note or anything?"

"Um," I started looking around the plant. "I don't see anything. This is exactly how we found it. We haven't touched anything."

"Okay, great." He took some notes, another picture at a different angle. "Do you have a camera or anything that shows the front door?"

"We don't." I looked over at Sawyer. He knew all the neighbors.

"Oh, um," he looked up and down the street. "This is such a quiet block. The only cameras I know of are on unit 1408, but they are too far down to see our door. Then unit 1506, but again, too far away to see the door. But either one could have picked up someone walking in the area or driving by?"

"Okay, that was 1408 and 1506?"

"Yes. 1415 might have one, too, but they are new, so I haven't gotten to know them yet." He pointed.

"Alrighty, I will go talk to them, but first," he pulled out gloves, donning them, then leaning forward to take the plant. "I will put this in the trunk."

"Do you need anything else from us tonight?" I asked.

"Nope, but whoever it is you pissed off, I would recommend you stop."

"Such a jokester, Raff."

His face went slack as his smile faded. "I'm serious, Jess. I've known you a long time and this might seem like an innocent gesture, but I think it is meant to send a serious message."

"You're right. Thank you." I flashed a weak smile. "I appreciate you coming out."

"Good night, folks." He tipped his head to the three of us, then put the plant in his trunk.

We turned to go inside.

"I'm writing oleander plant on the board," Vee said, running to the office.

"Add the comments from Darcy and Lolly," Sawyer called after her.

"I will!"

"You okay, friend?" He looked over at me.

"I honestly don't know. It was just a plant, but ... Raff is right. That was meant as a serious message." I rubbed at one of the scars from my car explosion. A reminder of what happens when I push too far.

"So, are you going to keep investigating this?"

I looked at him, really thinking. The smart part of my brain said no, but my heart had a different thought.

"Yes. Yes, I am."

"Well, alrighty, I am here for you." He wrapped one arm around me, hugging me to his side. "I love you, friend."

"I love you, too."

Chapter Ten

I hadn't found a reason to visit Caruso's yet, but I discovered they always have staff on hand to take in bodies. That meant if we even knew how to break in, we wouldn't be able to without risking someone being there.

"What are you thinking so hard about, Chef?" Noah said, coming to my station.

We hadn't talked much in the past few weeks. It was kept to mostly work stuff. I knew he was still dating April, Colt's sister, which made me so happy for both of them. They seemed to be a good fit. She was just silly enough to offset Noah's more serious personality.

It was the slow time of the day at the restaurant and close to shift change. Today, though, we were having a staff meeting where I would announce the winner of the cornbread. I already knew who the winner was, and I was excited to let them all know.

"Oh, just … nothing."

He studied me, so I tried not to fidget and look guilty. There was no reason to tell him about what I was thinking.

"Um, I don't believe you." He lowered his voice. "Does this have anything to do with Donna Overton?"

"I … I don't know what to say." I sighed, knowing I was busted.

"Just say I'm right."

I slowly nodded as my shoulders relaxed. It would be nice to bounce thoughts off of a friend, even if I didn't want him involved. I had a few things I wanted to run by him but hadn't bothered to ask yet.

"I knew it. Wait? You were cleared, or we were cleared. So why are you involved?"

"I found her there. It seems so sad that everyone is kind of writing her off because she wasn't well liked."

"Yeah, she had a reputation for sure, but I had met her a few times. She seemed sweet and not overly flirtatious, as people claimed."

"Yeah, I mean, I'm likely not her type," I chuckled. "But she didn't seem flirty to me either. She was simply a friendly person."

"My question stands, though. Why you?"

"Because *I can* isn't a good reason, right?"

"Maybe not for some, but I think it is!" He chuckled softly. "Are you using your clue board again?"

"We are. It is slowly filling up, but I think your experience could help with a few things."

"Me? Like what?"

"Accounting stuff. Business."

"Well, I guess I need to come by and see it."

"You should. Bring April. I can cook or we can pick something up."

"That sounds good. When?"

"Maybe tomorrow?"

"Perfect." He nodded and strolled off.

One hour later, I stood before my staff. They were waiting for the announcement of the winner of the cornbread contest and the student whose recipe would be added to our menu.

"Okay, that's all the business," I said after going through boilerplate stuff, like schedules, new time off policy, and other things. "Now for the moment you have all been waiting for, the announcement of the cornbread. It was close, very close. Even though I didn't officially vote, I know if I would have, it would have been an extremely difficult choice."

I looked over at Shayla, Jacoby, and Brooklynne. They smiled. Shayla blushed, looking down at her shoes. I knew this was important to her, to all of them, but unfortunately, there could only be one winner.

"I won't draw the wait out any longer. Jacoby, your cornbread is the winner and will now be included, along with Parker's biscuits, for everyone who orders."

Cheers and applause as everyone congratulated him. The other two didn't seem as upset as I expected. They simply shook his hand. Shayla caught my eye, and I could see a few tears. I walked to her side.

"It really was close. You should be very proud."

"The tears aren't disappointment. I'm proud of myself and of my classmates." She looked over at the winner, lowering her voice. "Jacoby was ready to quit school. A local drug dealer was heavily recruiting him. The money was tempting. But then you came to the school and gave us all hope. You saved him … and me." A few tears slid down her face. "Thank you."

"I am so happy that I could do that for all of you." As unprofessional as it might be, I gave her a hug. She quietly cried on my shoulder for only a moment before composing herself.

"Thank you, Chef. I better go get prepped for the dinner rush." She smiled and scurried to the kitchen.

I'm sure, like me, she found comfort in the routine of the kitchen.

I walked over to congratulate Jacoby and then gave Brooklynne some encouraging words.

With the staff meeting over and everyone either ending their shift or starting, I had nothing left going on, so I headed to the office to grab my stuff.

"Did Noah already leave?" I asked Cullen.

"Yeah, just a minute ago."

"Okay, great. I'm heading out. Call if you need anything."

"Great. Night, Chef," Cullen said.

"Good night."

I walked through the kitchen, but before I got to the back door, in came Noah. His face was creased with concern.

"What's wrong?"

"This." He handed me a paper. "It was on your car."

"On my car?" I took the paper.

I stepped out so I could look at my new car. Flashbacks of my other car exploding filled my mind, but the parking lot looked normal. Nothing seemed out of place.

"Yeah, I was walking to my car and saw something on yours. Given everything that has gone on in the last few months, I thought I should look. Some kind of threat."

"Bleep!"

I read it and yeah; it was definitely some kind of threat.

I hope you liked the plant and take it as a warning.
If you keep pulling at the threads of this,
you might not like what you find.

"Wow."

"You need to call Detective Upton, or at least your friend."

"Yeah." I pulled out my phone to call Detective Upton but hesitated a moment. He had told me not to investigate this after I had been cleared of the poisoning, but what was I going to say about this?

I exhaled as I pushed the button to call him.

After a moment, he answered.

"Upton," he said.

"Hey, Detective. It's Jessica Vasquez."

"Oh, yeah, hey, Jess. I am guessing this isn't a social call."

"You would be right. Did Rafferty tell you about the plant on my doorstep?"

"He did. Did you get another one?"

"No, this time it is a note on my car."

I heard him mumble something away from the phone that sounded a lot like son of a something.

"Are you at the restaurant or home?"

"Restaurant."

"I'll be right there."

I hung up and looked over at Noah. He crossed his arms, giving me a look that I couldn't quite read.

"What's that look for?"

"I didn't know you were so much trouble." He chuckled.

"I don't even know what to say to that."

"I'm not wrong though."

"No," I hung my head. "You're not wrong."

He stepped over, wrapping his arms around me. "You're a good person, though."

The hug startled me. He had never been much of a hugger.

"Thanks." I mumbled. "When did you get so touchy-feely?"

"What can I say? April has changed me." He ended the hug. "Do you want me to wait with you?"

"He might have questions for you, since you found it."

"Oh, true." He snapped his fingers. "We should check the cameras. I'll go download it."

He ran in while I waited for the detective. I stood there in the hot sun. This is not how I thought my afternoon would go.

Even though I hadn't seen anything unusual, I walked around my car, checking the doors, windows, and the tires. All looked fine. Of course, I didn't know much about cars, so who knows if anything else had been tampered with?

I heard a car, so turned to see Detective Upton pulling in, followed by a patrol car. I recognized the driver as Officer Tommy Roberts. I didn't know him as well as I knew Officer Rafferty.

"Oh, hey. Thanks for coming." I handed Upton the note. "Noah found it on my windshield."

Detective Upton looked around and then down at the note. After he read it, he handed it to Roberts who bagged it.

"Where is Noah?"

Before I could answer, the back door opened, and Noah came trotting out to join us.

"Here is a copy of the video footage, but it is highly disappointing."

"Why?" Upton asked.

"We had a special delivery, and the delivery truck parked right about … here." He gestured to the spot in front of my car. "There is a slight shadow but can't tell if it is related to the note. There is no other activity aside from employees coming or going. None go near her car."

"Well, thanks, we'll review it." He turned towards Roberts. "Why don't you go see if Dr. Vega's office got anything on their camera?"

Officer Roberts nodded, then turned to jog across the street.

"Dr. Vega is going to move if this keeps up," I whispered to Noah.

"For real," he mumbled.

Upton went to my car and looked it over. He pulled out some kind of bag from his car.

"I'm going to check for prints or any forensic evidence." He stepped to the car. "I should have brought a team," he mumbled as he got started.

Noah and I stood against the building, trying to stay in as much shade as possible, while we waited to hear what the verdict was and when we could go. It was a hot day, too hot to be standing in a parking lot, and ours felt like it was on the surface of the sun.

"I'm sweating my b—," He looked at me. "Well, just a lot."

I'm not sure when I got the reputation as some prude that can't hear bad or crude words, but that is what everyone thought. Honestly, though, I was okay with it.

"Yeah, it's miserable." I fanned myself with my hand. It did not help.

We watched mostly in silence as Upton worked and after fifteen or so minutes, Officer Roberts came jogging back across the street.

"Nothing great on their camera, either. It is like the person timed everything extremely well to not be seen," Roberts told the detective. "But I got what I could. We can check the street cameras when we get back to the station."

"Alright. I just finished up, so we can head back and get this to the lab for processing." He nodded to me. "I'll be in touch."

He turned to go, putting his bag and the evidence he'd collected in the back of his car. He turned to look at me, frowning deeply.

"Jess, I don't know why this keeps happening, because I already told you to stop looking into Donna Overton's murder, and you are doing that, right?"

"Um," I couldn't quite look at him.

"Stop. Stop today. No more of this, okay?"

His voice was so calm, yet full of authority. I knew he was serious, but I also knew that I had to see this through. Back home, I had a clue board that had the answer on it, and I just needed to put the pieces together.

"I don't know what to say."

He took a step forward. It could have been threatening, but it was more like a dad's move.

Standing in front of me, he looked me right in the eyes. "Say you will stay out of this."

"Okay." It was a compromise between what I wanted and what he wanted. I didn't say the words, so I didn't lie to him.

"I know that look." He ran his hand down his face as he sighed. "Fine, I can't control you, only warn you to stop. But if you do this, you might not be so lucky next time."

"I know."

He nodded and climbed into his car, giving me one final look before pulling out of the parking lot. Noah and I looked at each other.

"So, what time should April and I be over for dinner tomorrow?"

"Is six good?"

"That works. See ya tomorrow."

I watched as he got into his car and drove away. I stood there a moment, thinking about the past hour. Detective Upton was a good guy, but I know he had to protect the people of the town and he'd already saved me a few times before. I would take his words to heart and try to be a lot quieter and careful about who I talked to.

But wait, I hadn't really talked to anyone yet. Who knew I was looking into stuff? Just Aunt Rita.

I pulled out my phone and hit her number.

"Hey, Jessie!"

"Hey, Aunt Rita."

"Is everything okay?"

"Um, yeah, but I had a quick question." I paused. I hated asking her this question, but I had to know. "Did you tell anyone that I was looking into Donna's murder?"

"Oh, um, just our Bible study group. On Sunday before you kids got there."

Bleep!

"Okay, thanks."

"Is something wrong?" she asked.

"No, I just wanted to know."

"You would tell me if I caused you trouble, right?"

"Of course. Everything is fine."

"Okay, good. Love you."

"Love you, too."

I lied, so she didn't feel bad about the threats. At least now, though, I knew it was one of the ladies in that group.

Chapter Eleven

"Well, that was a nice visit. Your father really enjoyed seeing you, Jessie," Granny Ines said.

We had just left Milton County Prison where my father was spending his life sentence. I had been dreading this day since I agreed to it during Sunday dinner.

"Yeah, it was nice. He looked good." Better than last time I saw him, in a hospital bed, after being attacked by a fellow prisoner.

"What do you have planned for the rest of your day?" she asked.

"Oh, not much. I'm going to cook dinner, and a group of friends are coming over."

"That sounds fun. We're having an early dinner with our Bible study group. Joyce is hosting at her house."

I nodded. It was on the tip of my tongue to ask her who was going to be there. Would it be the same women from Sunday? But I knew the answer without asking. It would be. Several of them were on my suspect list, but as I didn't know all the ladies, I wanted to ask questions.

I also didn't want Granny to know about my investigation. She wouldn't like it at all, but if Aunt Rita had already told the group what I was doing, maybe Granny knew as well.

"Did any of the ladies say anything last time about Donna?"

"What do you mean, Mija? If they had a grudge big enough to kill her?" Her tone had me regretting the question.

"Yeah," I mumbled, embarrassed that I was even considering any of those sweet church ladies as suspects. Why would any of them kill someone?

"None of them would kill a fly. They are good Christian ladies. They go to church, do Bible study, give their time to charities and others. None would kill someone over something so silly as a *man*."

"I understand."

"Good." She looked out of the window. "Isn't Milton County so beautiful in the early fall?"

I knew that meant we were done with the topic of murder. We just enjoyed the ride home. I pulled in front of her house.

"I'm glad that you wanted to visit your father. Don't be a stranger. He really loves you."

"I will try to make more time for him."

She unlocked her front door, then turned to me.

"Don't poke at this murder, Mija. You know what happened last time." She looked me up and down. "I couldn't stand it if something happened to you."

A lone tear fell from her eyes. She was not the type to cry, so the one tear had a huge effect on me.

"I'll be careful."

"Umph, be a little more than careful." She leaned forward to hug me. "I love you, Jessie."

"I love you, too."

From here, I headed to the grocery store. I had a plan for dinner. It was going to be an Asian cuisine night. I grabbed all the ingredients for beef and broccoli, cashew chicken, and fried rice. I would also make egg rolls.

Every time I was in the store, people would greet me with praise. I always wondered if they did this to other chefs or if it was the fact that I was on television several times. They all knew my face.

We had just introduced the cornbread muffins alongside the biscuits. It had been a huge hit.

"So glad you added the cornbread."

"The cornbread goes perfectly with your alphabet soup."

"The biscuits were good, but the new cornbread muffins are my favorite!"

At the checkout, the cashier was also super chatty.

"Chef Jessica! Always good to see you in here." She started scanning my items. "What are you making here? This isn't for the restaurant, is it? New recipes?"

"No, just dinner with friends tonight. Doing a little Chinese inspired menu."

"I love it. Inspiring." She snickered at her little joke. "Get it? You said inspired and I said inspiring."

I smiled and nodded. I'd gotten it, but it was cheesy and awkward. She was sweet though.

She grinned. "Maybe I should do something like that for my dinner. Of course, I'll probably just pick up from Sushi 73, because I can't cook." She laughed again, then continued chatting away while I watched her ringing up all my items. "Do you have any coupons?"

"Oh, no."

"That's okay." She read my total. "Thanks for shopping with us! Enjoy your dinner."

I took the receipt and my groceries, then headed home. Once at home, I loaded the groceries, then went to look at the clue board. I wanted to double check that everything we knew, so tonight we had all the information.

When I got home from work yesterday, I had written Bible Study Ladies. Under that, I listed all the names I knew that weren't already on the board: Edie, Bea, Ruth, Joyce, and Elaine. Darcy, Lolly, and Tilly were already on the board separately.

"It has to be someone here, so how does the Caruso Funeral Home factor in? Or does it not?" I said to the wall. Of course, it didn't answer and none of the names screamed out to me. "I'm not going to solve this now."

I went to the kitchen to start my prep.

Right at six, there was a knock at the door. Vee ran to answer it.

"Hi, welcome!" she squealed. I turned as she hugged April. Vee always loved new people. "It's so good to see you again. How are you?"

"I'm good. Thank you all for inviting me." April said, smiling at all of us as they came into the kitchen.

"It smells amazing in here." Noah said, stepping in behind April.

"Thanks! Y'all want something to drink?"

"I'd like just water, if that's okay?" April said.

"Of course. Noah?"

"Same."

We got them set up with water and then I pulled the last egg rolls out of the pan.

"Alrighty, hope y'all are hungry." I gestured. "Plates here. Food there. Silverware is already set at the table."

"Guests first," Sawyer said.

One by one, we filled our plates with the saucy, savory food and made our way to the table. I smiled around the table as everyone started to eat. I could tell they were enjoying it.

"So, Sawyer, where is your girlfriend tonight?" Noah asked, giving me a look.

"She had to work. She's a nurse over at the hospital."

"She is?" I asked. Why didn't I already know that?

"Yeah, she's been working the night shift lately, so no gaming and no dates."

"Too bad. She seems fun," Noah said.

Sawyer laughed. "You were just hoping for a little drama, huh?"

"Busted." He grinned. "Yes, but she also had some different ways of looking at the clues, even if we didn't like it. Her opinions got us thinking about it differently last time."

"That's true. She just has a blunt way of putting it out there," I said. It wasn't my way of doing things, but that didn't mean she was wrong.

Vee nodded. "But she's nice once you get to know her."

"Aw, thanks, y'all. I have had moments of concern that she wouldn't fit in," Sawyer said.

"Well, maybe next time I'll get to meet her," April said with a smile.

She had a beautiful smile, and my heart skipped a beat as I remembered her brother's picture with the same smile. I still feel a bit cheated out of meeting a great guy.

Once dinner was eaten, Sawyer volunteered to clean up.

"I'll help you!" April said, grabbing plates and silverware.

"No, you're a guest," Vee and I said.

"But you all welcomed me and Jess, you cooked this amazing meal. It's the least I can do."

"Oh, thanks."

"Aw, it's our pleasure."

They got to work while the rest of us went into the office.

"Wow, I didn't realize you had so many clues already," Noah said with a whistle. He studied the different items. "Bible study group? Really?"

"Yeah, weird, right, but nobody knew I was doing this except my Aunt Rita. When I asked her about it, she said she had mentioned it during Bible study the other day. So, I am thinking, the person who left the plant, and the note, had to be in that group. Right, or am I crazy?"

"Um, you have a point."

"That's scary," Vee said. "We were in the room with the potential killer!"

I stared at her. She was right, and as I had known most of those women my whole life, I had known the potential killer that long. A chill ran down my spine. That was an awful realization.

I also thought of my Granny and Aunt Rita. Those women were some of their best friends. If one of them turned out to be a killer, it would break their hearts.

"What is this one about money laundering? Is that what you needed my help with? And what's this one, missing jewelry?" Noah asked.

"Well, it was suggested that a funeral home is a good place to launder money. They asked me for a paper invoice. We assume to limit an electronic paper trail. Then there are several scandals involving missing jewelry and items from people's coffins."

"Seriously?" He burst into laughter. "Y'all watch too many crime shows."

Vee's face fell at his words. "You don't think it could be something?"

Her sad tone caused him to sober up quickly. He straightened his back a little, then studied the board again.

"I mean, it could be something. Crazy things happen every day."

"So, what do you think?"

"Honestly? Hard to say but given what you said about the plant and note being sent after they were told on Sunday, that really points to someone in that Bible study group."

"Yeah, that's what I'm thinking too."

"That didn't get us very far," Vee said. "We narrowed it down to about nine ladies."

"Darcy and Tilly seem to have the biggest grudge against her."

"Though Tilly seemed to shift a little, since the affair was not with Donna," Vee pointed out.

"True," I admitted.

"But all of them said some nasty things."

"What kind of things?" Noah asked, with a little too much eagerness. He loved the drama.

"Just a lot of flirting with men, especially married ones," I said.

"And don't forget they said she was sleeping with Gio and Dimitri," Sawyer added, coming into the room with April following behind.

"There is no proof, but yeah, they said that."

"You are kind, Jess. Always looking for the best in people," Vee patted my hand.

"Did y'all come up with anything new?" Sawyer asked, taking a seat, his long legs stretched out in front of him.

"Narrowed it down to ... well, who we already thought. Someone in the Bible study group."

"I can't believe it. All those ladies are so super sweet. They are grandmothers and great-grandmothers," Sawyer said.

"I know." I plopped down into a chair, sighing. "I don't know if I want to solve this one."

Every head whipped to look at me, eyes bugging out.

"What?" I asked. "All of these women are dear friends to my granny and auntie. It's not only going to end badly for their own families but mine too."

"I have heard about the missing jewelry stuff," April said, out of the blue.

"You have?"

"Yes, in fact, it was Donna who suggested we not leave anything of value in the casket with Colt. She recommended we wait to add anything until the viewing and right before it was sealed." She choked slightly as she mentioned her brother.

She and I looked at each other, smiling weakly at each other. We have a connection now. A strange, almost "what could have been" connection.

"Do you know anything else about it?" Vee asked.

"Yeah. There was a friend of mine who lost her mother's wedding ring, a necklace, and a brooch. She said the last time she had seen her mother, it was all on her and she looked beautiful, ready for her service. They left for the evening and then the next day when they returned for the service, it was gone."

"Did they file a police report?"

"I'm honestly not sure. I'm sure they did." She pulled out her phone. "I'll ask her."

She typed out a message and then nodded when it was done.

"While we wait, does anyone want coffee, tea or anything else to drink?"

"Nothing for me," Noah said.

"I'm good as well. Thanks." Her phone chimed. "She says they did, but nothing came of it. Caruso's has a clause about lost items."

"That's frustrating. I'm sorry for her."

"Thanks." She typed out a quick message. "I just let her know that was helpful."

We all sat staring at the clues without saying anything for a minute or two. It wasn't helping me think any more clearly. All I knew was this would not end well for people I loved.

"Well, we better get going," Noah said. "Thank you for having us."

"Yes, thank you. The food was phenomenal, and the company and conversation were amazing." She leaned over to hug Vee, then me.

"We were so happy you could come. We should really do this more often." I said.

"We really should," she smiled, giving me one more hug.

After they left, Sawyer hopped on his video game, Vee pulled out a book, and I just went to stare at the clues I had already looked at a hundred times.

Nothing.

Chapter Twelve

I was walking to my car after what felt like the shift that wouldn't end. Our vendor was late with our food order, which put us behind in prepping. That set off a stressful day of playing catch up. We had several customer complaints, which was unusual for us, too.

All I could think about now was collapsing into my bed for an hour or two.

As I approached my car, I saw a familiar figure walking on the sidewalk across the street. It was Lolly, and she'd just come out of Dr. Vega's.

"Oh, Jessie, hello!" She waved and made her way across the street to me. When she reached me, she leaned up to hug me.

"Hi, getting your eyes checked out?" I smiled.

"Yes, these old eyes." She chuckled. "Getting hard to see at night, but otherwise, healthy as a horse."

"That's good to hear."

"Just getting off work." She looked around me at my car.

"Oh, yeah, just going to head home."

"So, Rita said you are looking into Donna's murder. Is that true?"

"Not much. I mean, yeah, I asked around a little, but nothing serious."

"Well, good. It can be dangerous." She patted my arm. "Well, I better get home. Gotta feed Ms. Tiggleton."

"Aw, I can't believe little Tiggy is still alive. I remember her as a tiny kitten."

"Yes, she will be fourteen years old next month. Us old ladies must stick together."

She waved as she crossed back to the other side of the street and made her way to a beige sedan. I remember when she bought that car. It was right after Ray died. She had made a big deal about it.

"I could never buy a small car before because my Ray was a tall, tall man." She had told me. "Now, this is my little car."

As tired as I was, I planned to stop at the store to pick up food for dinner. Why didn't I just suggest take-out? Or better yet, grab something from my place?

Nonetheless, I'd promised my friends tacos for dinner. Mine might not be as tasty as my granny's but they were pretty darn good.

As I was picking out tomatoes, I saw a familiar face. Darcy Whittaker.

"Oh, hey, Jessie. How are you?"

"Hi, Ms. Darcy. I'm good. How are you?"

"Good. What are you doing here?" She chuckled. "Before you answer, I know you're shopping. I guess I just meant what are you making?"

"Tacos."

"Yum. Do you make them like your grandmother?"

"I try, but they aren't quite as good."

"I'm sure you are better than you think. Well, I'll let you get back to it. Good to see you."

"Good to see you, too." I grinned, putting the tomatoes in the cart, waving to her as we both continued our shopping.

As I neared the registers, I heard a commotion from one aisle over. The sound of carts banging together echoed.

"Get out of my way!"

"You're in my way!"

There was another strange sound and then the sound of breaking glass. I joined the crowd as we all tried to see what was happening. That's when I saw Darcy ramming her cart into another shopper's cart. She grabbed eggs from the other lady's cart and started throwing them at her.

There was a gasp from not only the other shopper but the entire crowd.

Yikes, I guess it wasn't just Donna that Darcy had a problem fighting with.

"You hateful witch!" the shopper yelled as she grabbed Darcy's bread and threw it at her.

Darcy caught it and threw it back.

About then, the store manager stepped forward, trying to calm the situation. She got a face full of banana cream pie instead.

Someone called the police and soon they showed up. By then it was full on chaos as the two ladies had emptied each other's carts and half the shelves near them. They were covered in food and Darcy was missing half her shirt.

The responding officers were Rafferty and Roberts.

I backed up into the crowd so they wouldn't see me. The last thing I needed was to be linked to this mess.

Thankfully, they had their hands full trying to deescalate the situation. Once they had both ladies in handcuffs, the crowd cheered, which set off the ladies. They lunged at each other. The floor was slippery causing them all to fall, including both officers.

They all rolled around on the floor until a few bystanders stepped forward to assist them in standing. I suppressed a laugh as I saw Rafferty covered in food.

He pulled Darcy away from the other lady, so as to avoid any further fighting. They were making their way out of the store, when Raff looked over and saw me.

He flashed a mischievous smirk my way. I had no idea what he was thinking but it caused me to laugh.

I headed to the check out, paid for my groceries then headed home. I thought about the recipe that I'd use for tacos tonight. I'd need to break down the chuck roast and braise it until it fell apart.

My plans changed as I pulled up at home to find our front door open.

What in the bleep? I sat in my car staring, not sure what I was looking at. Had I left the door open this morning or had someone broken in?

"Lulu!" I flew out of the car to go check on my cat, not even thinking for a second that if someone broke in, they could still be there. I didn't care, I had to find my cat. She was an inside only cat but if the front door was open, she could have gotten out.

When I crossed the threshold, my brain didn't process that our house was trashed, and paint splattered everywhere. All I cared about was my cat.

"Lulu? Lulu, where are you?"

I ran through all the rooms on the first floor, looking in all her favorite spots, like the sunspot by our patio door and the windowsill next to the kitchen.

Next, I ran up the stairs. I saw that Vee's door was open, but I didn't stop there. Lulu never went in there anymore. Not since Vee kept finding her Funko Pop figurines knocked on to the floor.

My room was flipped upside down, but no Lulu to be found.

Bleep! Where is she?

Finally, I heard a muted meowing sound. Almost as if the voice was calling me.

"Lulu?" I ran to Sawyer's room. His room was almost as messed up as mine, but I couldn't think of that now. I had to find my kitten. "Lulu?"

A pathetic meow came from the closet. I whipped the door open and out darted my gray and white blur. She turned at the bedroom door to look at me, then ran out. Relief flooded my body that my baby was okay.

But now I had to deal with this mess.

I shot off a text to my roommates. Their reply was instant.

S: **Holy crap!**

V: **What did the police say?**

Me: **Nothing yet. I am calling them now.**

As I started to dial, I hesitated. I didn't know if I should call the detective directly or 9-1-1. In this case, I think the emergency number was the right thing to do, especially after Upton told me to stop any investigating.

"9-1-1 what's your emergency?"

"Someone broke into my house."

"Are you safe?"

"Yes."

"Are they still there?"

"No." I don't think so, but of course now my mind was playing tricks on me.

"Is anything missing?"

"Honestly, I don't know." I walked back downstairs to look around. Not being focused on finding Lulu, I finally took in the scene. It was horrible. "Everything is torn up and thrown around, so it is hard to tell if anything is missing."

"Okay," she took my address. "I have an officer in route. Do you want me to stay on the phone with you?"

"I think I'll be okay. My roommates are on their way home now."

"Okay, please call back if you need anything."

"Thank you."

I hung up and just stood there. I didn't know what to do. Tears were burning in the back of my throat. I began pacing around, taking in the mess.

This was going to take us forever to get cleaned up. I went into the office and my heart sank. Our board had been slashed and paint was splattered all over it. This was more proof that someone knew I was investigating Donna's death.

"Jess?" I heard Vee's voice call from the front door. "Oh, my gosh. Ohmygosh!"

"I'm back here."

I heard them walking, gasping, and Sawyer let out a few choice words as they came back to the office.

"Wow. Just wow," Sawyer said when he saw the office.

"Yeah," I held my arms out wide. "I guess this is another message for me to stop."

"Are you?"

I looked around at the mess. "I probably should."

"But you aren't?" Sawyer finished my thought.

"Probably not. I mean, how can I? Someone clearly doesn't want this to be solved. Someone with power."

"And a lot of extra paint," Vee added, her voice cracking. "Oh, wait? Where is Lulu?"

"She's okay. She's hiding right now, but I saw her, and she was fine. Actually, she had gotten stuck in your closet." I pointed to Sawyer.

"Really? I better go check out my room."

He ran up the stairs and a string of words came floating down as he took inventory of the damage in our rooms. Vee stepped forward, wrapping her arms around me, softly sobbing against me. Tears slid down my face as we stood there waiting for the police to arrive.

I hoped that the detective didn't hear about this, but it was a small department. I'm sure word would reach him.

Sawyer came down to check our living room. He righted the television and grabbed the remote.

"Oh, good, it still works. Just a little bumped and bruised, so to speak." He lightly chuckled. "Oh, and good, my game still works."

I assessed the kitchen. Nothing here looked damaged. Stuff was just strewn from one end to the other. It was a mess. My pantry had been emptied onto the floor. Flour, sugar, spices and the like would take us weeks to clean.

Didn't look like I was going to be cooking tonight or for a few nights.

Finally, there was a knock on the door. I exhaled, then walked to open it. In front of me were Officer Lupe Perez and Detective Richard Upton.

Well, bleep. I knew the detective would likely find out.

"Officer Perez. Detective. Please come in," I said, my voice nearly failing me. I knew I was going to get a stern lecture this time.

"Thank you," Detective Upton said, stepping inside. "Wow, Jess. They really got you good."

"Yeah."

Vee and Sawyer came into the room. Sawyer had Lulu in his arms. I didn't even see her come out of hiding.

She was purring and rubbing her head against his chest. I guess she blamed me for this, but obviously, this wasn't something I had wished for. I hope she isn't too traumatized and forgives me soon.

Detective Upton didn't budge from the foyer. He took in the scene from there and didn't say a thing for a full minute. Finally, he looked at Officer Perez.

"Go grab the kit and we will start gathering evidence. Call the station to see if someone is available to assist, and then call Gail about clean up."

"That's not—" I started to say, but he whipped his head around, giving me a death stare. "Never mind," I mumbled and tried to become one with the wall.

"Yes, Detective," she said. She stepped outside to put in the call.

"You. Tell me what happened here." He pointed at me.

My blood went cold. I had witnessed him being a kind and caring father and husband, a friendly and considerate person who loved his job and cared about the people of Dashwood. However, I had seldom seen this side of him. He had really lost all patience with me.

"I came home from work to find the front door open. I came in to ... well, all of this." I gestured around.

"Have you been looking into Donna Overton's murder?"

"Not since we talked about it last, and you said don't." I don't think I had anyway, so I didn't feel as if I was lying. I just couldn't remember exactly when he told me to stop. It had only been a few days or a week ago. I couldn't remember.

"Have you been able to tell if anything is missing?"

"Not yet." I looked at my friends.

"I checked my room, and other than being ransacked, it all looks to be there." Sawyer shrugged. "But look around, hard to say for sure."

"And no way this is at all related to anything with either of you." He eyed Vee and Sawyer.

"Well, I do work at the desk at the post office and people can get really angry, so who knows?" Vee said.

"Has anything like this ever happened before? Anything that could tie it back to a customer?"

"Um, no, nothing like this. I have had my car egged and notes left on it, but just angry words, no threats."

"And you, anything?"

"I had an ex-girlfriend once that keyed my car and slashed my tires."

I loved my friends. They were trying to help take some of the heat off of me, but I don't think it was working well.

"Uh-huh," Upton said, making a few notes. "What about your cameras? Do you have a recording, or is there a company who monitors that we can get footage from?"

We all exchanged a look.

"We don't have cameras," Sawyer said.

"I thought we talked about this. Get cameras, especially after this." Detective Upton eyed me up and down without a word. He was not happy with me, and frankly, at this point, I wasn't exactly happy with me either.

Thankfully, Perez came back in with the kit.

"Wright is on his way, and Gail will send a team over shortly."

"Great. I have the interviews done." He looked at us. "Can you show us the rest of the place?"

That's when I realized we were going to have to show him the office. My body froze, refusing to allow me to take a step. Vee and Sawyer exchanged a look, likely about the same thing.

"Right this way, Detective," Sawyer said, taking them first to the kitchen. They took pictures and Perez started looking for fingerprints and any other physical evidence. Next, he went to the living room.

"Thankfully, our television and my gaming system aren't damaged, at least not too bad."

"What's back here?" Upton asked, stepping into the office. "What in the world is this?"

B*leepity-bleep-bleep-bleep*.

I knew he would find it, but I really hoped we could have steered him away from this room.

Walking in, I saw that he was holding a few of the pages that had been ripped off the wall. I could clearly read "Bible Study" and "Oleander." He was not going to like this.

"I can explain," I started to say.

"I hope so, because to me, this looks like you are investigating using a murder board."

"Murder board?" Vee blurted. "We've been calling it a clue board."

"Well, yeah, I guess you could call it that. We call them murder boards or some call them suspect boards. It just depends on who and where." His tone softened when he spoke to Vee. He cleared his throat. "Were you putting anything together?"

"Not much. We had some suspects and some possible motives."

"But how did you know oleanders?" He held that paper out.

"I don't want to say," I whispered, trying not to make eye contact.

"It was Max Reeder, wasn't it?" Perez asked. Lupe had also gone to school with us. She was a year behind, but it was a small school. Of course she would know about Max. "He always had a crush on Vee."

"Me?"

"Yeah, he was always mooning over you."

"That's silly." Vee giggled. Of course, she had liked Max, too, but they had never dated. Both were too shy.

"So, Reeder gave you the information. Fine." He looked down at the pages in his hand. "Do you think you can recreate it?"

I don't know if my mouth actually fell open, but I was stunned. I looked at Vee and Sawyer.

"Um, yeah, I think we can," I stuttered.

"Okay, show us the rest of the place so we can get pictures and evidence wrapped up. Then our team can get in here and start cleaning for you."

We slowly made our way through the entire townhouse. After we showed them around, we left them to finish gathering pictures and evidence. We went downstairs to sit and wait. It was hours before they were done, and the cleaning crew showed up.

Without needing to be given much direction, they got to work scrubbing and cleaning top to bottom.

If we had to go through a break-in, this was the best part of it, having a clean-up crew do the work. But I felt so vulnerable and hurt.

If this was a message from someone I had grown up with, I was going to cry a lot. This was a huge betrayal.

Chapter Thirteen

While the clean-up crew worked their magic, Detective Upton helped us put the clue board back together, but this time in a more professional way.

"Like the real detectives do." Vee beamed.

"Well, I mean, kind of, but we don't really use these. Not like what you see in movies or TV shows. We might put something together to brainstorm, but not like this," Detective Upton explained.

"Really? That's disappointing."

"Yeah, I was a little bummed to find out that wasn't actually a thing, either." He winked at Vee.

She giggled.

He had us make several changes, starting at the top level. He suggested putting the motives first with the possible suspects under the motive that most matched them. Then any relevant clues under that.

It made a lot of sense this way, but I thought our way did, too. Vee had been so excited about it.

Now five days later, I was staring at it, mug of coffee in hand. Sawyer and Vee had left for work, and I had the whole day ahead of me with nothing planned. I probably should have gone to see my dad. That would have made Granny happy.

But instead, I planned nothing. It was going to be perfect and after the break-in, just what I wanted to do.

I shouldn't say nothing. My real plan was to lie on the couch, watching mindless television until it was time to cook dinner for my friends.

My phone rang. The display read Detective Upton.

"Good morning, Detective."

"Good morning, Chef. Are you busy?"

"No, not at all. What's up?"

"Okay, good. We found the person who broke into your place."

"You did? Who was it?"

"He claims it was a random attack. That someone hired him."

"Random? How could it be random if he was hired and who is someone?" I was stunned by the news.

"He didn't know the person. Said it was all done anonymously online." He paused. "I guess random attack is the wrong way to describe it, just that he didn't have a reason to do this to you. He was hired."

I couldn't process what he was saying. This didn't make sense to me at all. It was bad enough that this could have been someone I knew, but now someone was hired to harass and hurt me.

"Online? How do you even find a job like that? Thugs-R-Us?"

He laughed. "I guess, but honestly not sure. We do have him in holding now, but he will be released once he makes bail. He'll go to trial and be sentenced, but I can't guarantee he won't come back."

A chill ran down the full length of my spine at his words. "Yikes. Did he say he would?"

"No, he actually said he wouldn't. He said he only got paid for the one job."

"That's scary, but also kind of a relief."

"Did you get the cameras installed?"

"They're coming tomorrow to set them up."

"Great. He likely won't be released today. Either way, that will help and if someone does come back, we will get them on camera this time." He cleared his throat. "Anything new for the board?"

"No, not yet."

"Alright, well, I just wanted to let you know about the arrest. Take care."

We hung up. I processed what he had said about the break-in. I couldn't believe there were people online not only looking for people to do criminal things but people you could hire to actually do those things.

People are awful.

I finished my coffee and then took my place on the couch with my phone. An hour later, I wasn't sure where I ended and the couch began, when my phone rang.

"Hi, Auntie Rita."

"Hi, Jessie. This is your day off, right?"

"It is."

"Oh good," she said. "Did you hear about Darcy Whittaker?"

"Hear about what?"

"She got in a huge fight at Shop-a-way the other day."

"Oh, that. Yeah, I didn't only hear about it, I saw it."

"You saw it? Really?"

"Yeah, I ran into her the other day at the store, and I was wrapping up when I heard it. Things got wild. They were both covered in food, then Officers Rafferty and Roberts showed up and they got covered in food!"

We laughed.

"I wish I could have seen it." She chuckled. "Any news on the murder?"

"Unfortunately, no."

"Well, I hope you write down Darcy's explosive personality."

"I thought you and Darcy were friends." I was perplexed. They had been friends for years and I'd never heard Auntie Rita utter anything unflattering about her or any of her friends for that matter.

"Yeah, well, we aren't great friends. Plus, she has been angry lately at everyone."

I sat up. "That sounds juicy. Spill."

"After Bible study the other day, we stopped at Dashwood Teahouse for lunch. The server spilled one of the teas. Darcy jumped up, berating the poor girl. It was an accident."

"Oh, wow. Anything else?"

"Isn't that enough? It was so embarrassing for the rest of us."

"I'm sorry."

"Well, we can't kick her out of the group, but if we could, that would have been the breaking point. Then a day later, she had the blow up at the grocery store."

"It was a big blow out."

"Well, I have to get ready for Bible study group. I'll let you know if there are any more fireworks."

"I'll be eager to hear."

After we hung up, I stared at my phone for a moment. I didn't know Ms. Darcy well, but what I did know was that it all seemed out of character. Yes, she fought a few times with Donna Overton, but random people in public, that was too much.

I pushed up to go to the office. I grabbed a sticky note, writing 'anger issues' then stuck it under Darcy on the board.

"Shame. She always seemed so nice."

This had me thinking of the phrase 'crime of passion.' It was possible that she got in a fight with Donna, anger took over, so she killed her.

Wait? That doesn't make sense. Poisoning like that couldn't be a crime of passion. Stabbing her, shooting her, or even strangling could have been, but this had to take planning.

How do the sleuths on TV make this look so easy?

Okay, what if I think of what I know about each person?

Lolly has been a close family friend my entire life. She was a sweet person. Had two children and lost her husband a little over a year ago. She liked to crochet and garden, loved her friends, and was a good Christian woman. She did a lot of volunteer work.

Tilly was married, but her husband had an affair running off with her sister and my fifth-grade teacher. She owned a boutique jewelry shop. That was about the extent of what I knew about her.

The rest I knew even less about.

"Well, that didn't get me far."

Wait? I thought of Ms. Lolly again. She was big into gardening and was the president of the Dashwood Garden Club. That could mean she had access to an oleander or at least might know how to get them.

Bleep!

I didn't want to believe what was right in front of me. Nope, I was going to figure this out and it wasn't going to be my favorite babysitter.

Chapter Fourteen

I was sitting in the office at Caruso's Funeral Home, waiting for Regina to return. She called two days ago asking if I could cater for another funeral.

"I know you don't really do catering, and we did have someone else lined up, but they backed out. The widower has asked if you could do it. His wife loved your alphabet soup so much," she'd said on the phone.

"When is the service?" It had to be soon if they had all this set up and then they backed out.

"Next Saturday. Weekend after the art festival."

Ugh, I didn't want to do it on a Saturday, but fine. It might be okay.

"Okay, sure. When should I come back to talk about details?"

"Thursday?"

"I'll be there this Thursday about 3:30 in the afternoon. Good?"

"That's perfect."

That was on Tuesday. I had most of the menu worked out, staff changes made, and the extra food ordered. This time, I had Hannah and Ava lined up to assist me.

The main reason I agreed was to gain access to the funeral home. Perhaps if everyone was distracted, I could look around. If I got caught, I could say I was looking for extra napkins or something. Or that I got mixed up going to the bathroom or looking for their kitchen.

It wasn't a large commercial kitchen, but it was large enough that they could offer coffee, tea, and small bites at the services. However, on occasion, people wanted more, at least that's how Ms. Regina had explained it.

At the last funeral, we had been set up in the hallway in front of the viewing room or reception room. That is where she said we would be for this one as well. It made the most sense to me, as there was a lot of space to set up the long tables and still have people walk around as well as get to the reception room for the service.

Most funerals had their food service at a restaurant or a home, but as Donna had explained with the first funeral and Regina explained with this one, some people really liked it to just be at the funeral home. Everyone could just be in one place and not have to drive all over. Makes sense to me.

Regina was taking a long time. I didn't know how much time I had left before she'd be back, but if I knew, I could look around. Across from me were about eight file cabinets, on top of them were tons of file boxes. Should I get up and peek in a box?

I looked over my shoulder, listening for any noise from the hallway. Did I have time?

Now or never! I thought.

I started to stand up, just as Ms. Regina burst back into the room. Quickly, I pretended to be stretching and then sat down.

"Okay, sorry about that, Jessie. The printer got jammed. Twice," Regina said, her signature perfume engulfed me as she swished by me. She handed me the contract. "I wish Gio would find a new girl to replace Donna. I really hate doing this work. Anyway, that's the contract. Have a look and then initial and sign."

I nodded as I began reading the agreement. It was pretty straightforward.

"Wait? What is this about poisoning?" I tapped the paper.

"We are not liable if your food kills someone," she said, flatly.

"But I ... It didn't last time."

"Right, but just in case. You know, we have to protect our business, too."

"And I have to protect mine." As well as my reputation, but I left that part out.

"Okay, so you understand."

"Yes." Through a tight smile, I began initialing and signed the contract, handing it back to her when it was done. Was smoke coming from my ears?

"Great. Let me make you a copy."

She walked out.

I eyed the door as I sat there, waiting for her. Again, I eyed the cabinets and boxes. If only I knew where to look, I could grab something and shove it in my hobo bag. I always had an oversized bag. It was almost like my signature look, much like Regina's overpowering perfume that still lingered in the room.

Signing that contract made me less friendly and less likely to mind my own business. However, I was also not one to break the rules. It was a conundrum, but I suddenly knew that I had to try.

I stared at the door, trying to come up with a plan. There were the cabinets, the boxes on top, and the entire desk where I could pick something up.

Eying the door as I popped up, I darted to a cabinet. Peering in, I found that nothing was organized, nothing was labeled. I grabbed a couple of files, shoving them into my bag, and slammed my butt back into the chair before anyone could catch me.

I suppressed a laugh, but I had no idea if I had anything helpful. Would it show me if they were laundering money? Were they running some kind of scam to steal jewelry? I had no idea what I would find.

Regina came in with a huff. "Sorry again. That damn printer is so old. He really can't let go of anything."

I bit my tongue as I thought about her 80s inspired mauve pants suit and dated hair style she was sporting now.

"Thank you." I took my copy of the contract and stood to leave, trying to keep my posture and face as neutral as possible, knowing full well I had just stolen from them. "I'll see you on Saturday."

I walked as calmly as I could from the office, out into the main hallway, and out the front door. Stepping out the front door, I nearly ran right into Dimitri.

"Oh, excuse me. Oh, hi, Dimitri." I hadn't seen him. Did he know I'd stolen the file? I steadied my breathing, but inside I was a bundle of nerves.

"Hey, Chef. How's things?"

"Good. Good. How about you? Any new sculptures?"

"I have a beautiful collection that will be on display next weekend at the Art Festival."

"Well, I will be sure to stop by to have a look."

"Great. See you then." He went inside.

I looked once over my shoulder as I climbed into my car and drove out of there before I even put my seatbelt on. Nervous energy bubbled up as relief, bursting out with a hysterical fit of laughter.

"I can't believe I did that!" I shouted.

Reality set in a bit as I once again thought that there was little chance that I got anything of substance, but in a way, it felt good to stick it to the man, so to speak. If there was even one piece of paper that could point away from one of the Bible study ladies, it would be worth it.

I headed straight home so I could meet up with the company who would be installing cameras on both exterior doors and a few inside. They were recommended by Officer Perez.

"This is who I use. Can't take chances when it comes to protecting your family," Perez said.

"I agree with her. I got it installed at my mom's house after my dad passed. It has given me a lot of peace of mind," Rafferty agreed.

"I'd give a third vote. Highly recommend Security Geeks," Detective Upton said. "Especially working long hours with a wife and two children under two."

"Okay, that's who I use for the restaurant," I said, remembering that Colt had recommended them, too. "I think they're a good company."

I was so thankful they could come out so quickly. I called first thing on Monday morning, and they said they could come Thursday at four-thirty. I had ten minutes to get there. It was going to be close.

I would have had plenty of time, but Ms. Regina Caruso had talked my ear off then she had printer problems. It had taken me much longer there than I'd expected. I should have rescheduled with them, but it is too late now.

I pulled to the curb at my townhouse just as a work van parked across the street.

I hopped out and jogged up the steps to wait.

"Jessica Vasquez?" the worker asked.

"Yes. That's me."

"Great. I'm Corey."

"Hi, come in. Let me show you around."

I gave him a quick tour to show him where I wanted the cameras. He took notes and then made some recommendations regarding additional cameras and better placement.

"This window here looks like a good entry point if someone was looking to break in. I would highly recommend one here, especially given that you had that shooting. You might also want to get sensors to help with break-ins."

"Oh, you're right. I should get sensors on the windows. I didn't even think about that."

"I can add that for you. Someone in the dispatch office will be able to monitor and call the police. And of course, if you are home, you'll hear it."

"I think that sounds perfect. Thank you." I smiled. "What else do you need from me to get started?"

"Just a signature." He pulled a pen out, setting it on the clipboard he was holding. "Just here ... and here."

With that done, he got to work. The files I'd swiped were burning a hole in my purse, figuratively, of course, but I really wanted to see what I'd gotten. But first, I ran upstairs to change out of my chef's clothes. No shower until the security installer was gone or my roommates came home.

Lulu was asleep on my bed. She raised her head, blinking at me.

"Hello, Lulu. Are you talking to me yet?"

She yawned and snuggled back onto the bed.

Well, she didn't dart from the room today, so I'll take it.

I picked out one of Colt's old Neal Barney shirts that his sister April gave me after he had passed, pairing it with some yoga pants. Then I washed my face thoroughly. I may not be able to take a shower, but at least I could clean any grease and grime from my face.

Back downstairs, I grabbed my purse and set up shop on the kitchen island. Corey was by the front door installing the first camera. I could see him from here, so it was the perfect place.

Pulling out the files, I flipped open the first one.

It had several more manila folders inside it with names on the tab. I could only assume it was customers. I looked in the first one with the name *Bryce, Matilda* on it. The first page was the sales receipt for the coffin.

Casket: $1699

Custom color: $399

Satin lining: $199

Satin pillow: $99

Head Panel embroidered: $199

Grand total: $2595

That didn't include taxes. *Wow!*

Then, there was a whole other charge for the cemetery plot.

"Well, that's it. I will never die," I mumbled.

Then I got to a page that showed her belongings. It was worded as the body.

Cold.

When she'd come in, she had been wearing a nightgown and wedding ring. I read through each paper. The last page was a police report stating that all of her jewelry, including the wedding ring, was now missing.

Curious, what jewelry if she had been only wearing the wedding ring?

I pulled up the next file, and most of it was the same. Different burial packages and prices, but mostly the same documents, including a police report of missing items.

This could be something. If items were missing, maybe Donna knew who was doing it and was going to expose them. That was a motive.

I jumped up and ran to the clue board. I studied the various clues, taking it all in before adding the new information.

For the Carusos, we had stolen jewelry and money laundering. The Bible study ladies had jealousy and adultery above them. Then we had under each lady a time when they had a run in with Donna or made a comment that seemed suspicious.

Then, under all of that, we had oleander as the murder weapon.

Today I added the words 'multiple police reports' under Caruso's name. It fed the motive we had identified for them.

I stood back and took it all in. It was coming together. We had two good flows going. One was fueled by money and the other was jealousy. It was a good start.

The missing jewelry as a motive took the heat off of Lolly. I liked that. I wanted to go down this path. Gio killing her to conceal the truth. It could even be a yet unknown family seeking revenge for the missing jewels.

"Jess?" The security installer called for me.

"Coming," I looked at the board once before going to see what he needed.

An hour later, the cameras were nearly all in. He showed me how to update the app on my phone, so I could flip between the store and our house.

When Sawyer and Vee got home, they loaded the app as well. For them, it was only connected to our townhouse, not my restaurant, too.

"This is really neat. We should have done this years ago," Sawyer said. "It feels almost like a video game. Oh, look, there goes that old cat on our steps!"

"Look at him!" Vee giggled. "He doesn't even know we can see him."

Okay, my friends were goofy, but I loved them. I did have to agree with Sawyer though, we should have done this years ago.

We ended up watching it for hours. The only thing we saw was the neighborhood cat, a raccoon, and the new neighbors from 1415. They walked hand in hand, kissing once, and continuing. They didn't know we were watching.

"Do you think people sit in their house and watch us walk around outside?" Vee asked.

"Something to think about."

"It's actually a kind of creepy thought." I laughed, closing the app. I didn't want to be a creepy neighbor.

They kept watching, reporting what was going on. It was mostly boring stuff, but that was what we wanted. Boring was better than some hired thug breaking in to trash our house and scare me.

Plus, next time, I might not get so lucky with Lulu. I couldn't even think about what could have happened. The guy simply put her in the closet. She had hated it, but she was safe.

Chapter Fifteen

The Dashwood Third Quarterly Art Festival was this weekend. It started Thursday and would run through Monday.

That meant the restaurant was extra busy with tourists coming in from the surrounding cities to attend and check out all the vendors. This was the main reason I hadn't yet done a booth out there.

It was all hands on deck for this one, except for the three students. They had to work at their booth for the culinary arts school. However, for everyone else that meant no vacations, no extra days off.

Though we did allow everyone to work their normal schedules. Meaning they could still have their planned days off. For me, I would get to go to the festival tomorrow, Sunday, and then after we would go to Granny and Auntie Rita's for dinner.

The only drawback is that my Uncle Sully and his awful family would be joining, but Granny Ines had warned me that I better be there and play nice with them.

"She gave the same speech to Sullivan," Aunt Rita whispered to me.

It made me laugh.

"Chef, a customer would like to speak to you. Do you have time?" Skye asked.

I looked over my shoulder to where my lead line chef was working. She smiled, nodding that she could take over for me for a minute or two.

"I'll be right there. What table?"

"Eighteen."

"Got it." I finished the dish I was working on and then stepped over to the sink to wash up.

Then from there I headed to the dining room, which was full. That warmed my heart as I heard the happy customers enjoying their meals.

"Hey, Chef. Great food today."

"This cornbread is lovely."

"I enjoyed the soup of the day."

I thanked each one but then I realized who was at table 18. It was Ms. Lolly.

"Oh, there you are, Jessie."

"Hi, Ms. Lolly."

"I just wanted to tell you I was here enjoying the wonderful alphabet soup and these biscuits and cornbread. I had a little bit of each one."

"Well, we are glad you enjoyed it."

"I did very much." She smiled and patted the table in front of her. I didn't have time to sit, but I didn't feel I could say no either. "Ines told me about your break-in at your house. Scary times we live in."

"Yes, it was scary. I felt violated and vulnerable. Plus, I couldn't find my cat."

"Oh, no, Jessie, did you find her?"

"Thankfully, yes, but she has been mad at me since."

"I'm so glad you found her. Cats can be so funny, can't they?"

"Yes, they can." I looked around for Skye. She was the server for this table. I waved her over. "Ms. Lolly's tab is on the house."

The servers knew I would comp them any tips they missed out on when I did this.

This was partially out of guilt. I could not even picture her as a killer. It made me want to run home and rip her name off the board. She was a cat person. She couldn't be a killer, right?

"Great. Thank you, Ms. Lolly, for coming out to see us. I'll be around if you need anything else," Skye said, giving a big smile as she walked away.

"Jessie, you didn't have to do that."

"It is my pleasure, and just a little thank you for all that you and Mr. Ray did for me growing up."

"We loved having you with us. It was such a shame what happened with Tito. He was always such a good boy, but he had the hero complex. Always wanting to save and protect anyone around him, which I can understand and relate to that." She stood, pocketing a biscuit. "For later."

"I can get you fresh ones and some jam, if you'd like." I signaled to Skye before Lolly could reply. "Can you get a half dozen biscuits and blackberry jam for Ms. Lolly to go?"

"Absolutely."

"Well, isn't that generous? I will have them for my breakfasts."

Skye quickly returned, handing Ms. Lolly a white paper bag with our logo on it.

"Here you are. I got you all set up with some fresh ones."

"Thank you so much." She patted Skye's arm, handing her a ten-dollar bill then hugged me. "And you're sure I don't owe nothing?"

"I'm sure." I smiled down at her.

"Well, don't I feel special?"

With that, she turned and left.

"She seems sweet," Skye said but didn't wait for a reply as she turned to check on her remaining tables.

I watched as a new group came in and Jordan got them seated. I hurried back to the kitchen so I could relieve Hannah and finish my shift.

A couple of hours later, I stumbled out the back door, exhausted from the busy day, to find Dimitri Caruso leaning against my car.

"Hi, Dimitri."

"Hello, Jess."

"What's up?"

"Mom wants our files back."

"What files?"

He pulled out his phone and pushed play in a video. My face warmed as the screen showed me running to their cabinet, pulling out the files, and shoving them in my purse.

Bleep! I guess I wasn't as stealthy as I thought I was.

"Follow me to my house," I mumbled.

I can't believe this. Looking in my rearview mirror, I saw Dimitri's dark sedan pull out behind me. This was embarrassing.

My phone rang. It was Sawyer.

"Hey, Sawyer. What's up?"

"Want us to pick up dinner tonight?"

"Sure," I said. "By the way, the Carusos caught me stealing their files. Dimitri is following me to the house now so I can give them back."

"I'll be right there!"

Before I replied he didn't need to, he had hung up. Actually, I was relieved he would be there for me. I had no idea what Dimitri might do to me for stealing from them.

My phone rang again. This time it was Vee.

"Hey, Vee."

"Jessie! OMG! I can't believe that they busted you. We're on our way now. Do you want to stay on the phone with me?"

"No, that's okay. I think it will look more suspicious with you on the phone."

"Do you want me to call Raff or the detective?"

That was tempting, because again, this could be a dangerous situation. But it also showed disrespect to them. I am the one who stole, so technically, I was in the wrong.

"No, I think if you both make it home to meet us, I should be fine."

"Okay, well, we should only be a few minutes."

"Great. See you in a few."

Moments later, we all pulled up at the townhouse in near unison. I was so relieved to see them arrive with us.

Dimitri got out, stomping his way to my car.

"You called your friends?"

"No, they come home at this time."

"I'm not going to hurt you. Mom just wants the files back. No harm." He held up his hands. "I promise. You and I go way back, Jess, right?"

I pictured us at Lolly and Ray's years ago playing board games, playing tag in the backyard, and enjoying Ms. Lolly's fresh cookies. Good times.

"Yeah."

"Okay, that should count for something."

"It does."

Sawyer greeted Dimitri. Was it my imagination, or did Sawyer square his shoulders and puff up a bit? Vee came to stand next to me. What did she think she was going to do? She was probably half the size of Dimitri.

We all went inside.

Sawyer kept Dimitri in the front entry while I went into the office to retrieve the folders. We had all the information we needed from them now anyway, so it was fine.

"Here you are."

"And nothing is missing? Mom will kill me if anything is missing."

"It is all there. I promise."

"Whatcha want with these old things, anyway?"

"Nothing. I was just mad that they made me sign that contract with the clause about the poisoning, so I took something." Not a complete lie. It is what finally pushed me to do something.

"Well, that's silly. Both you taking this and them making you sign that."

"And she's not mad?"

"She thought it was funny. She laughed and laughed but then sent me to get them."

"Okay, well, I guess that's good. I didn't mean to cause trouble. I was just mad."

"Well, I can understand that. I would be, too." He saluted and went out the door. "Y'all take care."

We watched from our doorway as he hopped in his car and left without another glance. It wasn't until he was down the street that I exhaled. That was close, especially after whatever we heard in the woods that day.

"Alrighty, so maybe we overreacted, but glad it was nothing." Sawyer chuckled.

"Yeah, me too," I agreed.

"So instead of picking up dinner, should we just go out?" Vee suggested.

"Places might be crowded with the festival goers. I know my place was all day."

"That's true."

"I'll go grab us some pizza from Polly's Pizzeria. Let me just go change."

He sprinted up the stairs to change. We followed a bit slower. I hopped right in the shower.

Forty-five minutes later, we were all sitting around in the living room eating pizza and watching one of our television shows.

I was thankful I wasn't in jail for stealing or worse, killed for it. My restaurant was booming. Life was pretty darn good, and I wanted to keep enjoying it as drama free as possible.

Chapter Sixteen

I woke up excited about the day. We were heading to the Art Festival. They had advertised several new vendors. But the big excitement was that Neal Barney would actually be attending.

He rarely came in person anymore, sending instead an assistant or two in his place. I can't even imagine an artist being so huge that he could send someone in his place, but it had been this way for nearly two years.

I had been lucky enough to meet him prior to that. I had one t-shirt with his signature on it. I never wore that one. It was framed in the living room.

I headed for the bathroom. Then I pulled out my favorite Neal Barney shirt, looked at it, and decided it was too obvious. Instead, I pulled out an old garage band shirt.

It was still early enough that I decided to throw breakfast together for my friends. I pulled out mushrooms, onions, spinach, and sausage. I got the veggies cleaned and chopped while the sausage browned. Then I scrambled a dozen eggs. Once, the sausage was browned, I tossed the mushrooms and onion in, stirring them well. Finally, just before adding the eggs, I threw in the spinach. As it wilted, I poured in the eggs.

It was a masterpiece in the making.

"I love having a chef as a roommate," Sawyer's groggy voice said as he came in. He headed straight for a mug and the coffeepot, then kissed my forehead.

"Do you want toast with this?"

"Um, yeah, but I'll make it."

"Good morning, loveys," Vee said, coming downstairs.

"Good morning," we said in unison, then laughed at each other.

"It smells so good in here."

"Well, it's ready. Sawyer is on toast duty."

As we got our food and began eating, we talked about the day.

"I'm really excited to see the new vendors. They have a few new jewelry ones that I'm super excited to see!" Vee squealed.

"I saw Tilly's Creations on the list. I should probably check out her booth."

"She always has super cute stuff, so I would love to see what she has," Vee said.

"I was thinking for the murder investigation, but yeah sure shopping, too." Though I wasn't actually a big jewelry person. I loved that my friend was. It made it easy to buy her gifts. It was either her beloved figurines or jewelry.

"Well, I'm hoping Neal Barney is truly there. I would love to meet him again," Sawyer said.

"Me too," I said. "I'm hoping to get a signed print."

"Doesn't he sign each piece?" Vee asked.

"Well, yeah, but the second signature makes it more valuable," Sawyer said.

"And special."

He nodded and pointed at me.

"I'm a little nervous to see Dimitri, but also eager to see his sculptures." I thought about the interaction with him yesterday. A chill ran down my spine. That could have gone a whole lot differently.

"This is his first time going, right?"

"Yeah, that's what I heard."

"I hope that his mom isn't there today," I mumbled. "I do not want to see her at all."

They nodded.

We wrapped up breakfast, got ready, and started walking over to Albert Dashwood Memorial Park. It was another beautiful day. Friday's festival had gotten rained on, but today the sun was shining and there were only a few beautiful, fluffy clouds in the sky.

I could hear the music, people greeting each other, children laughing and squealing could be heard even before we could see the park. As we got closer, the spicy and sweet smells from the various vendor booths wafted across us, calling to us.

"Good thing you cooked breakfast or else you'd have to roll me out of here." Sawyer chuckled.

We latched on to Vee as we entered the crowds, so she didn't get swallowed up. Starting at the first booths, we started to make our way around the festival.

Vee spied the jewelry vendors, pointing us right to each one. Tilly's Creations booth was packed. We couldn't get close enough to it. We would have to circle back around.

My favorite things were always the paintings and wall art. I had many local vendors displayed in the restaurant. At current, I didn't have any wall space, but I still liked to look. Plus, I really wanted another friend for Luca, the elf, on my wall. He had been joined by Fritz, the dragon that I had acquired after Colt passed last year. Along with the Neal Barney shirts, his sister April gave me a dragon.

The pair greeted me each morning and always put a smile on my face.

"Chef, good to see you," a festival goers greeted.

"Thanks."

"We go to The Crock Pot each week!" his wife added.

"Aw, well, we appreciate your business and support."

This was the theme from many of the locals. At one point, I had someone overhear.

"Wait? Are you the chef at the Crock Pot?" a lady asked. She had a shirt that read *NANA IS MY NAME, SPOILING IS MY GAME*.

"I am."

"We stopped in there yesterday for lunch. It was excellent."

"That's great. I'm so glad you enjoyed it."

"We had the alphabet soup at the recommendation of our hotel. You put kale in it?"

"I do."

"I loved that. It wasn't bitter. Sometimes kale is bitter to me."

"We try to do our best."

"Next time we're in town, we are going back."

She smiled and moved on. I was glowing from all the praise. My dream had come true. I knew I was a good chef based on the cooking competition, but I was always scared of what the public might think. They are a different audience with different tastes than competition judges.

"You should be so proud," Sawyer whispered.

I smiled.

"Oh, there's Riley," Vee said. "Riley!"

She looked around, then seeing us smiled brightly.

"Hey, guys!" She stood on her tiptoes to kiss Sawyer, then hugged Vee. She eyed me, knowing I wasn't much of a touchy person with those I didn't know well. I smiled and hugged her. "I thought you didn't like hugs."

"I don't but it's festival day." We laughed.

Now we were a foursome, Vee and Riley giggled as they popped into another jewelry booth.

"I'm glad you like Riley," Sawyer said as we waited outside the tent.

"Yeah, there was just a lot going on when I first met her. She's blunt, but it's not like I haven't been around that my whole life."

"True, true. Your granny is as direct as they get."

"Yes, she is, but she loves me."

Thirty minutes later, we turned down an aisle and that's where I saw the sculptures. The pop-up sign read Twisted Metals and Jewels. On the table, were about a dozen little metal figures. He didn't have much on display, but what he did was stunning..

Vee tugged my arm so I could lean down.

"Do you think that's what he does with the jewelry?"

I took a long look at what he had displayed. It really could be. "Maybe so."

We moved closer to have a look. That's when I saw Regina. We locked eyes. Her face melted from a bright smile to an amused smirk.

"Well, Ms. Chef, didn't appreciate the wording in the contract."

"I'm sorry about that. I really don't know what I was thinking." I tried to laugh it off.

"Just don't do something like that again, or I will have to speak to your grandmother," She scolded.

I didn't know whether to laugh at that or be offended. I was a thirty-five-year-old business owner. Why would she tattle to my grandmother?

"I won't. Promise."

"Well, now that that's settled, check out what my little boy did. Aren't these fabulous?"

"They are." I had no idea what they were supposed to be. Most were literally just twisted up metals with random jewels affixed to them.

"This one is wind in motion," Dimitri said coming to stand near us.

Now that he said that I could see that he had bent the metal horizontally in rolling ripples. It was mesmerizing.

"Oh, yeah, I can see that."

"This one is a flock of birds. That one is a tree."

Now that he was pointing out what they were, it all made a lot more sense and seemed so obvious.

"They're amazing," Riley said, as she studied one of the pieces.

"Yeah, I love them," I agreed.

Then a thought popped into my head. I looked over at Sawyer and Vee. She nodded as if she could read my mind.

"How much is this one, the birds?"

"Really? Oh, um, two hundred?"

"Great. I would love to buy it. It's amazing and also, you know me, I love to support the local art scene."

He beamed with pride as he wrapped the item carefully and placed it in a brown paper bag with his logo on it. He then pulled out a card reader.

Once the payment had gone through, he handed me the bag with a huge smile.

"I really appreciate your support."

"Yes, thank you for this. It almost makes up for you stealing from us," Regina cackled.

I ignored her dig at my one indiscretion.

"Well, thank you for the wonderful piece. Keep it up."

"You know, I'm going to get one, too," Vee chimed in.

"Oh, my gosh, really?" Dimitri looked like he might burst.

"Yeah, this one. The tree."

It was several thin metal bars going straight up vertically which made up the tree trunk, then they curled up and out at the top to make the treetop. The metal bars seemed to be a mix of various textures and types of metal, like gold, silver, and maybe rose gold. Then it had jewels of all types attached to the curled part.

It was really neat looking but also suspiciously like old jewelry.

"That is one of my favorites. It is one-fifty."

"Great." She whipped out her credit card and waited for him to wrap it. "Well, thank you. I can't wait to get it home. I know just the spot."

He handed her the bag, then looked at Sawyer and then Riley, hopeful for another sale. They both simply smiled.

"Thank you for your purchase. I hope to have more things next time. It is sometimes hard to get enough made."

"Where do you get your inspiration?" Vee asked.

"Oh, just things I see. I love to go hiking in Milton County Park and then from there, I go to a lot of estate sales, consignment and thrift shops, and pawnshops. You wouldn't believe what people get rid of!"

"I bet." Vee smiled. "Well, best of luck."

We moved on. It wasn't until we were a few booths away and out of sight of Dimitri and Regina that Vee stopped me.

"So, the plan is to figure out if any of this is from the stolen jewelry, right?"

"Yeah, that's exactly what I was thinking."

"You think it could be?" Sawyer asked.

"Anything is possible. I mean, he has easy access to it."

"Wow, I am sorry that I had ever underestimated you guys," Riley said. "You do think outside the box."

"Yeah, I think we were all too quick to judge each other." I chuckled and then gently nudged her. She laughed, bumping me back with a smile.

We all stood there a moment, trying to decide which way to go next. I wanted to circle back to Tilly's booth, but I also wanted to see my employees and mentor at the culinary arts booth.

"I think the culinary arts school booth is that way." I pointed. "I want to say hi to everyone and see if Shayla has anything yummy to sell."

"I don't know. Jacoby's cornbread is my new favorite thing," Sawyer said. "I wouldn't mind a dozen or so of those muffins."

"I can definitely hook you up with those."

"Yes! I have said it before, but it is good to have a chef as a best friend."

We made our way over. As soon as the students saw me, and not just the three that worked for me, they all greeted me with shouts to try their food. I knew they all wanted to work for me. I really hoped I could hire more someday.

Shayla turned. When she saw me she gave a huge smile but I also noted a black eye. It looked as if she had tried to cover it with makeup.

"Oh, my gosh, Shayla. Are you okay?"

All eyes in the booth turned, and some of the students had frowns. I guess they knew, but I didn't.

"Um, yeah," her face turned red. "It's nothing."

I knew what that meant, but I wouldn't push it. If I got the chance, I would talk to her later and offer a safe place or at least an ear to listen. If I remember correctly, she was almost old enough to be considered an adult and could leave home.

"Well, what all do we have here?" I asked, plastering on a smile, even if my mind was now going to be on Shayla.

There were cookies, bars, fudge, and all kinds of different baked goods. I started loading up, being sure to label who had made each thing. My friends all did the same. Between the four of us, I think we bought half the booth. Not really, but it sure felt like it.

"And I know you love the snickerdoodles," Shayla said. "I made twice as many this time."

"Thank you." I leaned over. "If you need anything, and I mean anything, day or night, I am a phone call away. I mean it."

Tears formed in her eyes, but she smiled. "Thanks, Chef."

Changing my tone, I turned to all the students. "I can't wait to dig in."

I didn't see Duncan Jones, my teacher and mentor. He was the instructor for the culinary arts program.

"He ran to the restroom," Brocklynne said. She must have known I was looking for him.

"Ah, thanks. Well, good luck. I hope you sell out quickly."

We walked over to one of the many food booths to get drinks.

"Do you want to head over to Tilly's Creations again?" Vee asked.

I knew it was partially a selfish request on her part, but I really did need to check her out. I nodded, so we all trekked across the park to find that Tilly's was still packed.

"I don't care. I'm going in," Vee announced as she got in the long line and stood her ground as people tried to muscle over her.

Watching her, Riley and I jumped in, joining her. I was twice Vee's size, so people backed off when they realized we were together.

I didn't get the appeal of her jewelry though. It wasn't food. I would fight for some really good food. Looking at the shiny displays ahead of us, it looked like all the others.

But Vee and Riley were excited. They were pointing out different pieces, even though we were still too far back to really look. I'm glad that Vee had someone to enjoy this with.

"Oh, Jessie, hey!" Tilly's voice came over the crowd. "Come around this way. Oh, and Vee, too."

Vee pulled Riley along with us. When we reached Tilly, she hugged us both.

"By the way, Ms. Tilly. This is our friend Riley," I said.

"She's Sawyer's girlfriend."

"Nice to meet you, Hun." She smiled. "Did y'all see anything you liked?"

"A few things," Vee eagerly said.

They started looking at items, pointing out this type of stone or that metal, style of chain or wire. I had no idea. I simply watched, smiling when any of them looked my way.

Tilly pointed to the side. "Did you hear about Darcy?"

"Yeah, I was there."

"At the library?" Tilly asked.

"Wait? What?"

"What were you talking about?"

"I was at Shop-a-way when she got in a fight with that other shopper."

"Oh, wow, you got to see that. I bet it was a good one." She chuckled. "No, I was talking about when she got in a shouting match with one of the parents over a lost book."

"She is not having a good week or two, is she?"

"Yeah, it is like she suddenly snapped."

"What do you think caused that?" I had a few guesses, and I really hoped I was right.

"Honestly, she has always been an angry person, but I think she is just at an age where she just does not care what others say."

"Is that a thing?"

"Oh, yeah, some of us just handle it better." Tilly laughed.

It was on the tip of my tongue to ask if she thought that Darcy could have killed Donna, but Vee called her over to ask about a pair of earrings.

I marinated on what I knew about Ms. Darcy. She was definitely spiraling. It still didn't mean that she had poisoned Donna. That would have required planning, and I just didn't think that was Darcy.

Vee and Riley finished shopping. We thanked Tilly.

"So, do we go home now or do y'all want to see anything else?"

"What about your Neal Barney guy?" Riley asked.

"He wasn't at the booth." I frowned.

"Oh, well, yeah, I'm good."

"Me too."

"Well, let's go."

We left, Riley in tow. She would be going to Sunday dinner with us later. It would be the first time she would meet Granny and Auntie Rita.

I was a little nervous about that, mostly since my horrible uncle, aunt, and cousins would be there today. We had been lucky enough to avoid them since we had a huge fight a few months ago. We will see how today goes.

Of course, Riley might like a little drama that she wasn't involved in. I smiled at the thought, but also cringed inwardly. I didn't want any drama today.

Chapter Seventeen

After we got home, we freshened up and then drove over to Granny and Auntie Rita's house in near silence. I don't know why everyone else was quiet. For me, my mind was on Dimitri, but also Shayla for very different reasons.

I wasn't sure how or even if they could find out of the metals used in Dimitri's art were from anything missing from families, but I was sure going to ask Detective Upton. If he was telling the truth about where he got them, then this was a moot point.

Switching topics, Shayla's black eye. I knew most of the students in the culinary arts program came from troubled homes and backgrounds. I didn't know what any of them were going through, but I had some ideas.

I knew what I had been through as a child. Father in prison for murder. Mother pretty much washed her hands of being my mother. A stepfather who overstepped his role often. Then my two awful half-brothers. Spoiled didn't even begin to describe Christopher and Bryan. They were entitled jerks.

However, I knew my life was fairly easy compared to many others. Some were abused. Some had no food. They were in and out of jail themselves.

One of my friends from back then, Leighann, got pregnant. Then, when she was kicked out of her house, she started stealing to make ends meet. When she was arrested, she nearly dropped out of school, but Mr. Jones and his wife, Beverly, took her in. They helped her until she was able to graduate and got a good job. She's now married to a great man. He adopted her first daughter, and they had two more children together. They own a small chain of seafood restaurants in Florida.

Leighann was a fairly tame story compared to many I heard.

If I had to guess about Shayla, she was either being abused at home or maybe someone she was dating. It broke my heart. She was such a smart and sweet person. Tomorrow at work I would try to talk to her again.

Then I thought about Darcy. Boy, oh, boy, I didn't ever want to become that angry in life. I kind of felt bad for her. What was she going through?

"I'm kinda nervous," Riley said, breaking the silence.

"Aw, they are going to love you. Ms. Ines and Ms. Rita are sweet ladies," Sawyer said.

"Thank you for inviting me along." She turned to look at me. "I feel special."

"I'm glad you could join us finally."

Sawyer pulled the car to a stop at the curb in front of the familiar house. It had gotten a new paint color since the days when I lived here, but it still felt like home.

"At least we arrived before your awful uncle and aunt." Vee chuckled.

"And my cousins. Gag."

"Maybe they won't come."

But before we made it inside the house, they pulled up. Sawyer, Vee, and I groaned in unison. Riley chuckled at us.

"I can't wait to meet them all," she mumbled. "I have heard so much."

Uncle Sully stepped out of their large SUV. He frowned, but waved our way. Aunt Gina climbed out of the vehicle and frowned. Nova and Junior had their faces glued to their phones.

Good, don't speak.

Granny Ines opened the door, and yummy smells wafted around us. My stomach growled as it registered the smell of *arroz con pollo*. One of my favorite meals.

Oh, who am I kidding? I love everything.

"What are y'all all doing standing out here? Come on in."

"Thanks, Ms. Ines," Sawyer said, hugging her. "By the way, this is my girlfriend, Riley."

"Oh, nice to meet you, dear. We are happy to have you."

"Thank you, Ms. Ines." She stepped inside. "Oh, you have a lovely home."

"Aren't you sweet?"

She hugged Vee and me next, then stepped outside to greet the rest of the family who were standing on the sidewalk, not coming in. The screen door closed between us.

Granny's tone and body posture changed. "Mind your manners tonight, or I will not have you back in my house. Do you understand me, Sullivan?"

I don't think she meant for us to hear. Vee and I smirked at each other. Riley whispered something to Sawyer. They both chuckled.

"Oh, here are my favorite kids!" Auntie Rita giggled as she danced through the kitchen door. She was carrying a stack of plates, setting them down in the dining room before coming to hug us. "You must be Riley," she gushed. "It is so nice to meet you."

"Yes, thank you. It is nice to meet you as well."

She caught sight of Granny and the others outside. She leaned towards me for a hug.

"Oh, boy, Sully is here," she grumbled.

"Yeah, I'm looking forward to it, too."

"Edie and Lolly are going to join us today. Hopefully, with them here, my brother will be on his best behavior."

"We can only hope."

We took seats in the living room and waited for Granny and the rest of the family to join us.

"Can I get you kids some drinks?"

We placed our orders with her. She nodded.

"Thanks, Ms. Rita. I'll help you," Sawyer said.

They went into the kitchen. I peeked out the front window to see Granny Ines still talking to Uncle Sully and Aunt Gina in the yard. Nova and Junior kept smirking at each other. Whatever Granny was saying, it must be juicy. I wish I could hear it, but was also glad I couldn't.

"So, this is where you grew up?" Riley asked.

"Yeah, and it hasn't changed much." I looked around at the familiar walls.

Some decorations had changed, but not much. It was still decorated in the late 70s artwork with dark wooden framed orange and brown prints and the macrame olive green owl. I had named him Martin. There was a China cabinet with various ceramic figurines in it. I remember having to dust those as part of my weekly chores.

They had gotten new furniture in the late 80s. It was green and red plaid, like Christmas every day. I used to love sleeping on it. It was almost magical. I slept so well on it.

"It looks cozy and nice." She smiled. "And it smells amazing in here."

The front door opened, and in came Granny, Uncle Sully, Aunt Gina, and my cousins. The cousins were back to faces glued to cell phones. They went straight to the dining room and took seats.

"Granny? Why are there so many chairs in here?" Junior bellowed from the other room.

"We're having Edie and Lolly over."

"Who?"

Granny rolled her eyes and didn't answer him. She joined us in the living room, sitting in her favorite chair. It matched the couch and had an ottoman. There was a second one that Aunt Rita usually sat in.

Aunt Gina went to the kitchen to find Rita. I could hear them talking about dinner.

"Hi, Jessie, how is work?" Uncle Sully asked through a tight smile. I could tell he was trying.

"It is going well. We had a big weekend with the festival."

I wouldn't know how well until after Noah tallied everything up, but I had a feeling it was going to be good.

"That's nice." He nodded. "And you must be Riley, Sawyer's friend."

"His girlfriend," Riley corrected with a sweet smile.

"Oh, yes." Sully looked over at Granny to see if she approved of his politeness.

She was speaking quietly with Vee, so she never heard him trying to be polite. They were talking about Vee's family. He sighed and plopped down in Rita's chair.

Aunt Rita, Sawyer, and Aunt Gina came back in with drinks, which broke up some of the discomfort and forced conversation. This was going to be a painfully awkward dinner.

"Did you make it out to the festival?" Aunt Rita asked me.

"Yeah, we did. Lots of great vendors."

"I got this beautiful bracelet." She shook her wrist out so we could see the shiny bangle.

"Oh, did you get it from Panda's Beaded Jewels?" Vee asked.

"I did! You have a good eye."

"I bought a few things from her."

"I got a ring from her," Riley added.

There was a knock at the door. Uncle Sully popped up to answer it.

"Hi, Ms. Lolly. Hi, Edie. Come in," he said, politely holding the door wide for them.

"Thank you, Sully," Lolly said, shuffling in.

There was a round of hellos and introducing Riley to the newcomers.

"Well, are we ready to eat, then?" Granny asked, standing.

"Yes," everyone agreed.

We moved into the dining room. I sat between Edie and Vee with Aunt Rita on Edie's other side. Lolly was at the end next to Granny, with Sully next to Lolly. Aunt Gina was next to Granny, Nova, and Junior next with Sawyer and Riley rounding out the seating.

We passed the platters of food around. Everyone heaped their plates with the beautiful chicken and rice, enchiladas, tamales, and rice and beans.

"This is chicken and rice?" Riley whispered to Sawyer, blushing when she realized everyone looked at her.

"Yes, arroz con pollo. It is one of Ms. Inez's specialties," Sawyer said.

"Well, aren't you a sweet boy, Sawyer?" Granny bubbled with pride. "I hope you enjoy it too, Riley."

"I'm sure I will. It smells amazing." She took a tentative bite, chewing slowly. A smile formed on her face as she finished chewing. "Oh, wow, that *is* amazing!"

Chuckles rose from around the table.

After, we ate mostly in silence, only speaking when we needed something passed, like salt or tortillas. It wasn't until everyone started to fill up that the conversation picked up again.

"Jessie, I saw your mother at the store the other day. She said they had a nice vacation in Florida," Edie said. "Has she shown you the pictures?"

"Um, no. I don't get to talk to her much."

"Oh, that's a shame."

"Edie, you know that Margot pretty much dumped Jessie here with us. She isn't much of a mother," Granny said.

My throat tightened. This is not what I wanted to talk about or even think about.

"Oh, I'm sorry, Jess. I am so insensitive sometimes." Edie smiled weakly. "I should have remembered."

"It's okay." I shifted in my chair.

"Well, then, let's change the topic," Lolly said. "How are things at the restaurant?"

I felt like this was a question I was always being asked. It was a fair question, I supposed.

"It is going well. Busy this weekend with the festival and people are loving the cornbread we recently added." I smiled over at Auntie Rita since it was her idea.

"Those are yummy, but I like the biscuits better." She grinned. "Anything new with Donna's murder?"

All eyes turned to stare at me. I couldn't answer this honestly, so I would just do the best I could.

"Oh, no, I gave up on that."

Lolly shrugged. "Too bad. I thought the Crime Fighting Chef could solve it."

Nadine, a blogger who writes *Dining with Nadine*, gave me that nickname after I solved Earl's, my sous chef, murder. She'd come in and done an interview with me on not only the restaurant, but on solving the murder.

I hadn't actually solved it. Just stumbled into the restaurant as I was being robbed. I still got credit for it, even from the police.

"Ha, yeah, that was just dumb luck." I chuckled, looking around, begging with my eyes for someone to change the topic. They weren't quick enough.

"I don't know," Lolly said. "You always had those mystery books as a child."

"She does like those crime shows, too." Granny Ines pointed out. "But that's exactly what got her in trouble."

I really didn't want to talk about this. It was a dangerous topic, and I couldn't trust several people at this table not to cause drama.

I'm looking at you, Uncle Sully and Aunt Gina, I thought.

"I ... I can't argue with that. It did get me into trouble."

The group chuckled at me.

"Did you make it to the art festival this weekend, Ms. Lolly?" Sawyer asked. He used his most charming voice.

Thank you, Sawyer. I smiled at him. He winked.

"Oh, no, I don't go to that anymore. It is lovely, but I'm too old to walk around with the crowds and the heat." She laughed. "You'll learn one day."

"I got this bracelet," Aunt Rita said. She was extremely proud of her bracelet.

"It's gorgeous." Edie examined it.

Conversation shifted and never went back to me or Donna's murder. I was thankful for that because I didn't have answers and I also didn't want to be the center of attention.

But I could feel Ms. Lolly's eyes on me for the rest of the visit. Did she know that I had her at the top of my suspect list? If she did, she should know that I was trying everything to get that suspicion off of her and onto anyone else.

But my gut just screamed that she did it. I just couldn't figure out why. The fight at Mr. Ray's funeral didn't seem like a big deal, but maybe I didn't understand it fully.

After dinner, I messaged Detective Upton about Dimitri's art. I didn't know if they could do anything, but it was worth trying.

He replied he would stop by tomorrow after work to look at them.

Me: **I get home around 3:30**

Detective: **Perfect. I'll be there.**

Vee leaned against me. Normally, I sat in the front seat because I was tall and the back seat wasn't comfortable, but with Riley along, it felt respectful to let her sit next to Sawyer.

"What did the detective say?" she asked through a yawn.

"He'll come over after I get home from work."

"Did he say whether he could tell if it was from the stolen jewelry?"

"No, he didn't say. I hope so. It could really help solve that problem, at least."

"Do you think solving this will help with the murder?" Riley asked.

"I hope so."

Chapter Eighteen

The next morning, I woke with a start. What had woken me up? I looked around, but nothing seemed out of place.

Lulu stood on the bed, staring at me.

"Did you wake me up?"

She meowed at me.

"Are you hungry?"

She meowed and started kneading her paws on the blanket.

"Well, okay, let's get you some food."

She jumped down, running to her food bowl. I filled it with her dry kibble, then pet her head to tail. Even though she took the credit for waking me, I couldn't shake this eerie feeling. Was it a dream? It's happened to me before.

A really intense, vivid dream would wake me, and the feelings stayed with me all day. However, most of the time, I could remember what the dream was about, and I would spend the rest of the day processing and trying to make it make sense. This time, I have no idea what it was.

I went to the restroom, washed my face, and then headed down for some coffee. Maybe that would make me feel better.

As I sipped at my coffee, I tried in vain to remember the dream. I just couldn't recall it and the dread stayed in my soul.

"Morning," Sawyer said, shuffling into the kitchen. His hair was wild, but he was dressed for work.

"Good morning," Riley said, coming up behind me. "Oh, coffee!"

"Mornin', y'all." I smiled.

He got her a mug and pointed her to the creamer in the fridge. He would have to buy more for Vee if Riley used too much. I laughed quietly at the thought.

"Do y'all have time for me to make breakfast, or do you need to get going?"

"I have to get to the hospital. I just have time to gulp down some coffee," Riley said, smiling. "But next time, I would love breakfast. He is always bragging on it."

They smiled at each other.

"Yeah, raincheck for me too," Sawyer said.

A moment later, a flustered Vee came jogging down the stairs. She exhaled when she made it to the kitchen.

"Ack, I overslept a little bit. Are you ready to go?"

"Yep." Sawyer inhaled the last of his coffee. He kissed my head. Vee hugged me quickly and then the three of them left.

I had a few minutes before I needed to get dressed, so I made myself a couple of pieces of toast and scrambled eggs. Simple, but it should keep me going through my shift at work.

As I ate, I looked at the two sculptures we'd bought from Dimitri. I really liked them, and while I wanted to solve the murder and theft at the funeral home, I also wanted to keep the piece. It was stunning with the twisted and turned metal.

Maybe my uneasy feeling was because of the two sculptures. Perhaps I knew this could solve something which could put a target on me. Perhaps it was because of my nickname, The Crime Fighting Chef. Even Ms. Lolly had used it.

It felt just … wrong for her to call me that, or anyone to call me that. I hadn't done much. Just dumb luck.

It didn't matter, I couldn't do anything with the sculptures or to lessen the dread until I spoke to Detective Upton this afternoon. Even then, he'd need time to research the jewelry.

I finished up my breakfast then got dressed for work. Checking my reflection in the mirror, I smiled. I still wanted to pinch myself daily that this was my job.

When I stepped out, Dimitri was leaning against my car. My blood froze. I should have checked the cameras before coming outside. Lesson learned. I will do that from now on.

"Oh, hi, good morning," I sputtered out.

"Good morning. I come in peace!" He laughed, holding his hands up. "I just wanted to come to thank you for supporting me. You and Vee really made my day yesterday."

When he mentioned the artwork, I realized his intentions were innocent, or at least somewhat. Was I right to think that those had put a target on me in some way?

Still, my heart started beating again.

"You're welcome. I really liked your work."

"I haven't had the best luck making a go of this new career. My dad doesn't support me."

"I'm sorry. But your mom was there with you."

"Oh, yes, she's the best. Dad and I just have a ... complicated relationship."

"How so?"

Dimitri looked me up and down as if only just taking me in. He frowned.

"You're going to work?"

I looked down. "Um, yeah."

"Sorry. I should let you."

"Wait? Dimitri, if you ever need to talk, I am available. I do know a thing or two about having a complicated relationship with parents."

He blinked a few times. "Oh, right, your dad is in prison. Tough."

"But also, my mom."

Once again, he stared at me. It was unnerving, even if he seemed to be here on friendly terms. I shifted my weight as I waited for him to respond or leave.

"Look, all I will say is I don't like the way he does business, and he wants me to take it over someday. That's not what I want and definitely not with how he does things." He paused, looking around. He leaned closer to me. "Some of the things he asks me to do are unethical. *I don't like it.*"

I thought back to the day Sawyer, Vee, and I were hiking and we saw his car at the park, and heard strange sounds in the woods. Was this what he was talking about?

"I can understand," I said, without truly understanding, but I had seen enough true crime to come up with some ideas.

He smiled. "Thanks. Well, I better let you get to work. By the way, love your food."

"Oh, I didn't know you'd come in."

"A few times, but mom goes in about once a week. She'll bring me something back. My mom is a saint."

"Now it is my turn to thank you and your mom for your support. It means a lot to me."

He beamed with pride. He put out his fist, so I bumped it with mine. I never understood the gesture, but it didn't matter, he seemed happy with our bonding moment.

With that, he left. I watched him leave before I climbed in my car to head to work. That could have gone a lot differently. He scared me and, with his hints at what he did for his dad, confirmed my fears.

The rest of my day was uneventful, but the sense of dread never stopped. Did that mean I was close to solving this? My head said no, but my gut said maybe. One name kept rising to the top, but I couldn't let my mind even accept it.

At three, I said goodbye to my staff and rushed home. I wanted to at least get changed before Detective Upton arrived. I slid my car to the curb ten minutes later.

I ran upstairs, hopped in the shower, and took the quickest one I had ever taken. Once I was out, I dried and threw on a t-shirt and yoga pants.

There was a knock at the door, just as I made it downstairs. *Good timing.*

Swinging the door open, I said, "hey, Detective. Come on in."

"Hi, Jess. Thanks." He stepped in. "Oh, are these the pieces?" He pointed towards the kitchen island where the two sculptures sat.

"Yeah, we bought two, so we had a good selection of jewels and metals."

He picked up the birds, examining it closely, turning it in his hands. Setting that one down, he then picked up the tree.

"Um, it looks like this one might have an inscription on it, but I can't quite read it."

I leaned over to see where he was pointing. I hadn't noticed that before.

"It says *'My ride or die. Partner for life.'* Interesting."

"Yeah, definitely interesting. I can use that to cross check the reports to see if any of the jewelry had that inscription." He pulled out his phone and began taking pictures.

"Do you need to take them with you?"

"Oh, I didn't know if you wanted me to do that, since you bought them."

I nodded. That made sense. "I fully expected you to take them, but hopefully, if they don't lead to anything, we can have them back. I actually really like them."

"They are really nice. If this doesn't turn out to be nefarious, I will look into getting one for myself."

"So, what now?"

"I guess that's it. Do you have any new clues?" He hitched his thumb towards our office.

"No, nothing. It is like everything dried up."

"Um, yeah, I'm not getting much either. Do you mind if I look at the board for a moment? Just a refresher."

"Not a problem."

We walked back to the office.

"You added about the police reports? How did you get that information?" He pointed.

"Yes, I did." A warmth spread over my face as I remembered how I got that information. "I'm embarrassed to tell you how I got that bit, but—"

"I hate to even ask, but spill."

"I was at Caruso's because they want me to cater another funeral, and well," the blush deepened. "I stole some files from the office."

"You did what?" His voice rose, but then softened. "Do you still have them?"

"No, Regina noticed and checked the security camera. She sent Dimitri to fetch them from me."

"Yikes, be careful. I can't prove anything yet, but the rumor is they have a few dangerous business practices." His tone sent a shiver down my spine.

I already heard that bit of gossip, but to hear him confirm that he'd heard it, too was validating.

"Yeah, I have heard that. I will be careful."

"This does make sense though, but I still feel like we are missing something."

The front door opened.

"Honey, I'm home!" Sawyer's big voice sounded.

"Back here."

"Oh, hey, Detective," Sawyer said, coming in with Vee on his heels. "Anything new?"

"Not yet, but maybe if those sculptures show something." He did the finger crossing sign.

"We are hoping it helps," Vee said.

"Me too. I don't normally want citizens getting involved in these things, but this action is low risk and could be a huge help to us."

"Do you know how long before you'll have an answer for us?" Vee asked.

"I don't, but we have an inscription on at least one of the pieces, so that could help us a lot."

"Really?"

"Yeah, on that one you bought, it said *'My ride or die. Partner for life,'*" I said.

"Oh wow, that's cool." Vee giggled. "I'm going to look."

We all followed her to the kitchen island where the pieces still sat.

"I see it. How did I not notice before?"

"Oh, yeah, I see it, too." Sawyer looked over her shoulder.

Vee looked up at the detective. "Are you taking them?"

"Yep, I am going to see if our team can find anything in the various reports that match." He picked up the sculptures. "Well, thanks for this. Maybe we will at least solve that."

"I hope so," I said.

I held the door and then watched him walk to his car. Turning back to my roommates, I smiled a hopeful smile and did the fingers crossed sign. That's the best I could do at this moment. Hope and wait and keep trying to connect the dots.

All lines pointed to one path, one person and if I actually named the person, I would hurt my family and friends deeply. I was grasping at other things to try to deflect. If I solved the stolen jewelry case, maybe it would take focus off of the murder, then I wouldn't have to break my grandmother's heart.

I just couldn't figure out where she had gotten the oleanders, but the President of the Garden Club could likely get all kinds of things and know how to hide them from sight.

Please let me be wrong.

Chapter Nineteen

"Hannah, can you place that tray at the end?" I directed.

We were setting up for the funeral that I didn't want to do. Mostly because of the clause in the contract but also my own embarrassment at being caught stealing from them.

It turned out the couple went to church with Granny and Auntie Rita. The wife, Esme, was part of my Granny's Bible study group. I had met her a few times but could never remember her name. Granny and the entire Bible study group would be at the service today, so for many reasons, I wanted to do a good job, so I didn't let down Granny and her friends.

"Here?" Hannah asked.

"Perfect." I turned to Ava. "Do we have more plates in the van?"

"Yep, I was just heading out to get more. You want them on that table?"

I turned to the one behind me. "Yeah, yeah, that works. Thanks."

Alonso, the widower, came over. "Oh, Chef Jessica, this looks so good. Thank you."

"We're happy to offer our services."

"Esme would love that you were doing this for her service. She loved your soup." He smiled as his eyes watered. He wiped them.

"I brought a large pot of it in her honor." I pointed to the warming pot.

"Oh, Chef, thank you." Tears fell a little faster, though he had a huge smile on his face. I picked up a napkin, passing it to him. He wiped his eyes. "Thanks. Well, I will get out of your way, but I wanted to say a huge thank you before the day got started."

I wanted to ask him if she had been wearing jewelry or anything of value, and if it was missing today. But I didn't want to paint a bigger target on me or upset him unnecessarily.

We got back to work and by the time the first guests started to arrive, we were ready.

"Oh, Jessie, darlin', everything looks so wonderful," Auntie Rita said, leaning over to hug me. "You have a real talent here."

"Well, thank you, but I couldn't have done it without my wonderful employees." I gestured to Hannah and Ava. They smiled.

"Good job." She waved as she went to speak to Alonso.

Granny came into the room then. She smiled my way, but then looked around. I guess she was looking for the widower as well. He was standing outside of the reception room greeting guests.

I watched as she approached him. They had a few words, a soft laugh through a few tears, and then an embrace. She turned to look at me again before going into the reception room.

I was a little surprised she didn't come over like Aunt Rita did, but that's also not why I was here. We were here to serve food to the guests, not mingle with my own family, but I just wanted her to be proud of me.

I shook off my insecurity to focus on guests, smiling at everyone who came to get food.

"This is that amazing soup, isn't it?" a lady asked as Ava handed her a bowl full.

"It is." Ava grinned.

"This is my favorite!" another lady shared. She grabbed a biscuit and made her way to the reception area.

I hadn't been to many funerals, but this service was being done a little differently at Alonso's request. He wanted people to mingle and visit, all while eating good food.

Regina had mentioned that the family wanted it informal.

"He said nothing stuffy or formal. That wasn't who his wife was," Regina had shared. "She loved food and wanted people to enjoy something delicious while remembering her. At least that's what he said."

I could only nod. It sounded like a perfect memorial to me. When I die, that's what I want too. Something simple, comforting with good food.

An hour later, the guests were all in the reception room listening to the priest, family, and friends speak about Esme Pena. We could hear bits and pieces.

"Well, everyone is busy. I'm going to go drop this in the office."

"Can you bring back some more ice from the kitchen?" Ava asked, as she checked temperatures and food levels.

"Of course."

I took the invoice, leaving them there. When I reached the office, I took a deep breath. Last time I opened this door, there was a dead body. I knocked quietly.

"Come in," Regina's voice called out.

Oh, thank goodness.

"Hi, Ms. Regina. I just wanted to drop this off."

"Thank you." She smiled, taking it from me. "I don't need to pat you down for my files, do I?"

My face warmed. "Um, no, I am sorry about that."

"Don't worry about it, and that's the last I will mention it. I swear, but just had to take one more cheap shot at you."

"Ha. Good one." I tried to joke, but it sounded flat to my own ears. "Well, thank you. I'll let you get back to it."

I backed out of the office, then headed for the kitchen, breathing a sigh of relief that Regina didn't make a bigger deal out of the files. Pushing the door to the kitchen open, I saw Lolly crushing something in a mug.

I froze as our eyes locked.

"Well, hello, Jessie," she said. "I guess you know my secret now."

She let out the most wicked laugh. Not a cackle and not a snicker, but one that sent ice through my veins.

"You? You killed Donna?"

"It was supposed to be Gio, but stupid Donna. Oh, so stupid Donna. She picked up the wrong cup." Lolly smiled, as she added coffee to the mug she was holding. The one with the crushed up something in it. "No real loss though. Nobody but you cares."

She let out another evil laugh. "Now, today, I will finally get my revenge on him."

"Revenge for what?" I was already in this. I might as well know the reason.

"For me." Dimitri came around the corner with a gun pointed at me.

"What in the bleep? What is going on?"

They looked at each other before bursting into laughter. Again, it was an evil, manic laugh.

"What am I missing?" I sincerely asked.

"What you are missing, dear, is that this is my grandson." She patted his cheek, smiling.

"What? How?"

"My son had an affair with Regina and the result of that affair..." She gestured to Dimitri.

"Seriously? Does Gio know?"

"Yes, and I have been trying to get him out of the picture ever since."

"And I have stopped you every time." Regina came in another door, holding a gun.

I felt so ill prepared for this, whatever this was. I looked from gun to gun. Mother versus son versus grandmother, though she didn't have a gun. No, she had a mug filled with poisonous coffee. I didn't have any kind of weapon.

"Regina, you are such a fool. I am doing this for you and Dimitri. Gio is into bad, bad things. He is going to get you both killed." Lolly wagged a finger at her. "I'm just looking out for you."

"You just want me to marry Alex. I'm not going to do that," Regina said. "I love Gio, even if I had a moment of weakness thirty-five-ish years ago."

"But he is going to get my grandson killed with the things he is asking him to do."

"Like what?" I couldn't help but ask. I was caught up in the drama, forgetting that one gun was trained on me.

All eyes turned to me as if I had grown three heads. I guess they didn't want to share as they got back to the family drama.

"Dimitri knew what he was getting into," Regina argued.

"I did not," Dimitri protested. Regina shot him a look. "Okay, I knew a bit, but burying ... things in the woods, being an enforcer, were not what I thought I was signing up for. I thought ... I thought I was going to learn about the funeral business, not embezzling and laundering."

Oh, we were right about what was happening here. But I made sure to keep my surprise hidden and my mouth shut.

"Your father explained all of that to you," Regina said.

"Gio is not my father!"

"Alex hasn't even been there for you."

"Because of you. You picked Caruso over *my* father. What was he supposed to do?"

"He should have fought for me. Gio fought for me, so yeah, I picked him."

"With no consideration for me or what I would want?"

"I did think of you. I gave you a wonderful life. I support you and your dreams. You have wanted for nothing. I gave you everything. Who got you all the materials for your sculptures? Who runs interference between you and your father?"

"That is *not* my father!" He turned to face her. At least the gun was no longer pointed at me.

"Look, this isn't getting us anywhere," Lolly said. "I need to get Gio to drink this."

She started to walk out, but Regina stepped in front of her.

"Oh, no, no, no." Regina grabbed the mug, spilling it all over and knocking Ms. Lolly off balance. "Leave Gio alone."

Dimitri jumped in to steady Lolly before she could fall. In the process, he dropped the gun. It went off, shooting a hole in the wall next to me. I jumped, screaming, and covering my ears. Then came screams, shouts, and yells from down the hall.

Footsteps thundered down the hallway, and chaos erupted around us. Someone picked up the guns. Someone else secured Dimitri, Lolly, and Regina until the police arrived.

They brought in nearly a dozen officers.

Raff stepped forward. "Well, what do we have here?"

"I solved the murder," I smiled.

"Not exactly." Rafferty smirked. "Sounds to me like you stumbled on it."

"Okay, maybe, but I was close to solving it." I didn't add that I was in deep denial that the prime suspect was one of my grandmother's lifelong friends and one of my favorite babysitters. I hadn't even processed that fact fully yet.

He chuckled and walked away. I turned to see Granny walking towards me.

"Did you know?" Her voice cracking.

"I ... I wasn't sure, but ..."

"You should have told me." She turned, leaving me standing there, words caught in my throat.

Even though it was just words, I felt like she had slapped me across the face. I knew this would hurt her deeply. That is why I couldn't solve this, at least not on purpose. By accident, yeah, that I'm good at.

Chapter Twenty

It had been two weeks since the trio had been arrested. Regina had been bailed out the next morning. Dimitri had to wait another two days. They were both being charged with felonies for larceny.

Lolly had no bail set for her. They had considered her too dangerous.

Once in police custody, she confessed, or really it was more like bragging, about all the people she had killed over the years. She had been responsible for being the Morality Killer and the reason that oleander became illegal in town.

She called it avenging those without a voice. Even her own son-in-law had been a victim. Apparently, Diane had been in an abusive relationship and one night she ran to Lolly's house with her little boys. She was bloody and beaten; the boys were terrified, so Lolly took matters into her own hands.

Diane called Aunt Rita in tears and hysterics when she found out.

I wasn't there because Granny wasn't speaking to me, but Auntie Rita called me to tell me about it.

"Did you hear the news?"

"No, what?"

"Diane called me. She gave me all the information on her mother's ... um ... crimes."

She then told me all about it. The murders, the crimes of the victims, and poor Diane's life since her mother killed her husband.

"She said while she was glad, she was free of him, that is not how she would have wanted it to happen."

"Sure, sure."

"She wanted him to face charges, be punished for the rest of his life."

"I can understand that."

"Yeah, so Lolly is still in jail. No bond. They want to keep her there. She says that's fine, says she's gonna die soon, anyway."

"That sounds like Lolly. Is Granny still upset with me?"

"She isn't really upset with you. More with the whole situation."

"Am I still uninvited to Sunday dinners?"

That was the ultimate grudge for Granny. No Sunday dinners. Sawyer was more upset than me.

"Sadly, yes, for now, but I know she will forgive you. It is you. Her sweet granddaughter."

"She has another granddaughter."

"Well, you are her favorite."

"Funny how she shows it."

"Give her time. Her longtime friend has been charged with murder. Err, multiple murders," Aunt Rita said. "She loves you, though."

I wanted to ask her about Ms. Darcy but as I had long suspected, she was not involved at all. I guess it was just an angry at the world thing.

Detective Upton finally confirmed that yes, in fact, the stolen jewelry was from the funeral home. That is why Regina and Dimitri were being charged.

"It isn't possible to give the pieces back to the families, but at least they have closure on what happened."

"And what about Gio?"

"Claims he didn't know. Regina says he didn't, but I'm not sure." Detective Upton sighed. "I know there is more happening over there, but I can't prove anything yet."

"Yeah, I think so, too." Not just because they told me there was, but I already had my suspicions about it. That wasn't my problem. "So, I assume we don't get the sculptures back."

"Sadly, no. They are now evidence."

"Well, glad we could help."

But now it was Sunday, and I finally got the call from Granny that we were invited. She'd forgiven me faster than I thought. Sawyer was super excited.

We pulled up five minutes before we were due.

"Are you ready for this?" Vee asked from the back seat.

"I think so," I mumbled. Granny had never been mad at me before. Not like this, so it was all new to me.

Granny stepped out onto the porch.

"Well, ready or not," Sawyer said as he swung his long legs out of the car.

"Hi, Granny." I waved as I made my way up the walkway.

"Hi," she grumbled.

I kissed her cheek. A greeting I had done hundreds of times. She frowned and then opened the screen door wide for us. I exchanged a look with my friends as we stepped in.

"Oh, the kids are here." Auntie Rita danced into the room, a platter in one hand. She set it down and then came to greet us with hugs. "I missed you three. It hasn't been the same without you."

"Can I speak to you?" Granny said, pointing towards her bedroom.

"Yes, of course."

I dragged my feet a little as I followed her to her room. This reminded me of the few times she would discipline me as a child. She'd tell me she was disappointed, which would make me cry. I didn't want to cry today.

She walked to the far side of her room to look out the front window. This was her move. It built suspense and set my teeth on edge. She let out a long, deep sigh, turning slowly with tears in her eyes.

"I am so sorry that I was mad at you." She softly started to sob. "I wasn't really mad at you. I just felt so blind-sided by … everything. Then to find out that you knew, I just was hurt."

"Yeah, well, I suspected, but I was still connecting the dots. Plus, I didn't want to believe it, but all signs pointed to her."

"I'm so proud of you, Mija. I know that couldn't have been easy." She wrapped her arms around me.

With that business out of the way, we went to have a nice dinner and put the unpleasantness behind us. I was so thankful that it was solved, and we could once again move on with our lives.

THE END

Before you go: If you loved Cornbread and Coffins, be sure to visit my website to sign up for my newsletter (if you haven't already) and to stay up to date on new releases and other bookish things.

When signing up, you will receive **Chef Jessica's Alphabet Soup Recipe** as a free gift. I have "had" it, it is yummy. (Okay, so obviously, it is my recipe, but still, I recommend it!)

Continue to the next section for this book's recipe!

www.ejwheltonwrites.com

Recipe:

I am not exactly a fan of cornbread (me and Noah that is. Did you catch that in the story?), so I dreaded finding a recipe. It was going to mean lots of testing and tasting cornbread. However, when I got to this recipe, it was a winner. I found the original recipe on Pinterest and then made it my own from multiple recipes.

I hope you enjoy it as much as I did. This will now be my go-to if I need cornbread.

Cornbread:

Ingredients

For cornbread:
1 cup milk
4 tablespoons melted butter
2 large eggs
14.5 ounces creamed corn (1 can)
1 cup cornmeal
1 cup all-purpose flour
3 tablespoons sugar
1 teaspoon salt
2 teaspoons baking powder
1 teaspoon baking soda
1 teaspoon black pepper
1 cup chopped jalapeno peppers + sliced jalapenos for topping (like less heat? Don't include seeds or omit this completely)
1 cup shredded cheddar cheese (freshly grated it best. I do not use pre-shredded cheese for recipes)

For topping:
¼ cup unsalted butter, melted
3 tablespoons honey

Instructions
Heat oven to 375 degrees F (190 degrees C).

Whisk together the milk, melted butter, eggs and creamed corn in a small bowl.

In a larger bowl, combine the cornmeal, flour, sugar, salt, baking powder, baking soda, and black pepper.

Mix the cheese into the dry ingredients to coat with flour/cornmeal.

Pour the wet ingredients into the dry ingredients and stir together.

Stir in the chopped jalapenos.

Pour the batter mixture into a lightly oiled 9 x 9 baking dish and bake for 25-35 minutes, or until the cornbread sets and an inserted toothpick comes out dry in the center.

Meanwhile, combine the topping ingredients (1/4 cup melted butter and 2 tablespoon honey) in a small bowl.

Poke holes in the top of cornbread gently all over with a fork or knife. Pour honey-butter mixture all over cornbread. Let sit for 5 minutes before slicing and serving. ENJOY!!

Author note:

Another fun book done.

I loved how this one turned out. It kept me on my toes from start to finish. Yes, believe it or not, the characters hijacked this one big time. I really thought it was going a different way. In the end, I am thrilled.

Thank you to my editing team and BETA Readers. To my cover designer, another beautiful cover!

And my patient husband who has been the best taster tester of all things. He deserves a medal. He is going to enjoy the next things I have planned. Chicken and Dumplings, eclairs, and then falafels.

Thank you, dear reader, for your support and for reading my stories. I have many more to come with Chef Jessica and friends.

www.ejwheltonwrites.com